"You're not going alone," Bella interjected.

"And you're not coming." Marco was fast to reply.

"It's my house. You can't tell me I can't come. I know it better than anyone. If there's something wrong, I'm the one who has the best chance of seeing that."

"If this masked man has come after you in the daylight, then going home to a place he's been inside of isn't the best idea."

Marco wanted to help to solve this now.

Still she shook her head.

"I am no more safe here than I would be there. But at least there I have a chance to find something that might be able to help us stop this guy from ever coming for me again and hurting any of y'all. I'm going." She looked Marco square in the face. "The only choice you get to make now is if *you* want to come with *me*."

Finally Marco caved.

And he did so with a smile that put heat into her veins.

"Yes, ma'am."

SEARCHING FOR EVIDENCE

TYLER ANNE SNELL

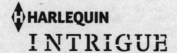

This book is for my father and the shed he built from scratch.
Both are in this book and both make me insanely proud.

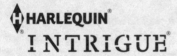

ISBN-13: 978-1-335-55524-3

Searching for Evidence

Copyright © 2021 by Tyler Anne Snell

Recycling programs
for this product may
not exist in your area.

This edition published by arrangement with Harlequin Books S.A.

For questions and comments about the quality of this book,
please contact us at CustomerService@Harlequin.com.

Harlequin Enterprises ULC
22 Adelaide St. West, 40th Floor
Toronto, Ontario M5H 4E3, Canada
www.Harlequin.com

Printed in U.S.A.

Tyler Anne Snell genuinely loves all genres of the written word. However, she's realized that she loves books filled with sexual tension and mysteries a little more than the rest. Her stories have a good dose of both. Tyler lives in Alabama with her same-named husband and their mini "lions." When she isn't reading or writing, she's playing video games and working on her blog, *Almost There*. To follow her shenanigans, visit tylerannesnell.com.

Books by Tyler Anne Snell

Harlequin Intrigue

The Saving Kelby Creek Series

Uncovering Small Town Secrets
Searching for Evidence

Winding Road Redemption

Reining in Trouble
Credible Alibi
Identical Threat
Last Stand Sheriff

The Protectors of Riker County

Small-Town Face-Off
The Deputy's Witness
Forgotten Pieces
Loving Baby
The Deputy's Baby
The Negotiation

Manhunt
Toxin Alert

Visit the Author Profile page at Harlequin.com.

CAST OF CHARACTERS

Marco Rossi—As the newest hire to the Dawn County Sheriff's Department, this deputy is ready to help those in need after the corruption that tore through the town. Yet after his run-in with a beautiful stranger, all of his attention and determination set on keeping her safe from a stalker who will do anything to get to her.

Bella Greene—After her life takes her on an unexpected path back to Kelby Creek, Bella settles into her hometown hoping for less mess. But when anonymous emails and letters start showing up along with mounting danger, she can't escape the fact that someone wants her and they'll do whatever they can to keep her away from the one deputy who can protect her.

Carlos Park—A long-time deputy with the sheriff's department, this Kelby Creek local becomes a partner who Marco might finally be able to trust.

Grant and Val Greene—Bella's father and brother, who, along with her, own and operate a small construction business called Greene Thumb and Hammer.

The Masked Man—A man who shows up after several unusual occurrences happen around town and to Bella.

Prologue

If Bella Greene had met the newest hire at the Dawn County Sheriff's Department six months ago, things would have been much different.

She would have seen the man getting out of his fast-looking car, wearing jeans that were a grace from God and a smile that would have been a knee-wobbler and started the conversation out on a good note. One that might have included some light flirting and mild self-consciousness, considering she wasn't wearing her usual work clothes but instead a party dress and heels that brought her that much closer to Heaven.

Under different circumstances, she would have been Southern-belle polite, laughed a little at her own misfortune and tried to make a new friend, something she'd been lacking since she'd come back home to Kelby Creek, Alabama.

Under different circumstances.

But the note clutched in her hand, so tightly

that her nails bit into her palm around it, had taken whatever her normal reaction might have been and flung it away into the darkening skies above them.

Bella didn't care that the man looked good—olive complexion with complementary dark eyes, heavy brows, jet-black hair that was styled back and a sharp nose and jawline, all which made her instinctively think of her childhood crush of A.C. Slater from *Saved by the Bell*—the fact was she didn't know him.

He was a stranger.

A tall, dark and handsome stranger, but a stranger all the same.

And out beside the county road with the town-limits sign in the distance and a broken-down truck behind her, Bella didn't want a stranger.

Not after the note she'd found in her tool bag just before he'd pulled over and not after the hang-up calls, anonymous emails and *the box* from the last few months.

Bella Greene was only for trusting two people right now and she'd been on the way to meet them in the city for a small-business award ceremony before her truck had decided it wanted to strand her just as night was falling with a storm rumbling in the distance.

"Hey there."

The man's voice was deep and low. Strong,

smooth. He moved across the two-lane with purpose. When he made it to the dirt shoulder she was standing on, his gaze flitted across her.

She might have thought he was checking her out—she *was* wearing her party best after all—but then she zoomed her focus out from him and remembered that, while in one hand she had the note, in the other she had a wrench.

A wrench she was holding like a bat, ready to swing.

"I'm assuming you're having some car trouble?" His gaze swung behind her to the propped-open hood of the old Tacoma she'd purchased after the family business had started making decent money. It was rusted and worn but was a miracle when it came to transporting building materials from the store to a jobsite. Even now it held a truck-bed toolbox filled with nails, screws and plastic shams.

None of which she could use as a good weapon on the fly.

Hence her trusty wrench.

"I'm okay. I'm waiting on my brother to show up," she lied.

The man didn't seem convinced. He motioned up and over to the thundercloud, which was getting dangerously close. That and night was not a great combination for a broken-down vehicle in the country.

"Is he getting here soon?"

Bella tightened her grip on the wrench.

She was doing fast math now.

If he came at her, how long would she have to counterattack? How hard and fast could she get the wrench against him to give her the lead?

Bella slid her foot back a little on reflex, trying to strengthen her stance like a little kid readying for someone to come her way during red rover.

The man didn't miss the move.

His eyes widened a little.

He held out his hand and surprised her with a laugh.

"I'm only asking because the radio just said the storm is moving fast and I know it's fall but I've heard enough tornado talk in the South to be afraid of the possibility of them year-round." He put his hand into his back pocket and nearly gave her a heart attack as he pulled something out.

Then the object he'd reached for was out in the waning daylight and the logical part of Bella's brain forced that fear to pause.

It was a badge.

He held it so she could see it.

"It's also my sworn duty to make sure everyone in the county is as safe as can be."

"You're a deputy?"

He nodded.

"The newest at the Dawn County Sheriff's Department. My first official day is tomorrow but—" he nodded again to the approaching storm "—I thought I'd stop to help."

This time Bella took a moment to eye the same cloud.

Her brother, Val, and their father, Grant, were nowhere near her. Her mother was far away with her aunt in Huntsville and, as Bella had been keenly aware of recently, her own friend circle had shrunk to acquaintances from growing up. And even those few acquaintances she'd grown apart from since she'd fled town. Then there was Bob Sanders's tow company half an hour out. And, last she checked, he had prices that were more problematic than his pickup time.

"My name's Marco. Marco Rossi."

Bella snapped back to the present and away from her list of people she hadn't yet called.

Deputy Rossi returned his badge to his back pocket but didn't make any move to come toward her. In fact he held up his hands in defense before she could respond.

"And, listen, I get it. Creepy guy you don't know approaching you on the side of the road when your truck is disabled is a bad look. That said, I can't in good conscience just leave you stranded out here. So I'm going to go back to my car and wait until your ride gets here. *But* if they can't or the storm is too quick, I wouldn't mind at all giving you a ride into town. I mean, Kelby Creek is so small, it's not like anything is out of the way. Sound good?"

Bella hadn't expected that. Still, she nodded.

It was all Marco needed.

He said, "All right," and went back to his car. Instead of getting in it, he leaned against the opposite side and faced the field.

Bella loosened her grip on the wrench.

But not the note.

She was still clutching it when she spoke to her father and Val on the phone, also saying she was going to have to miss the event, and still had it pinned against her palm when the rain started.

It was only after she locked up her truck and approached the deputy that she moved the note to her bag.

"Could you take me to Crisp's? It's a restaurant off Main Street."

Marco was quick to nod. He was also quick to open the passenger-side door for her. Bella caught a scent of cologne that reminded her of the woods as she hesitated in front of him.

"I took a picture of your car, your license plate, and sent it to my dad and brother. I also described you to them and told them your name.

I'm supposed to call them in ten minutes, which is how long it should take to get there."

Marco surprised her again and laughed.

"I can appreciate the caution."

Bella took a breath and slid into the passenger's seat.

She settled her bag on the floorboard.

She might not have been holding it in her hand anymore but Bella still felt the weight from it.

And even though she was watching as the rain picked up and hit the windshield, three words written in red ink were as clear in her mind as when she'd first read them.

Hello there, friend.

HE WATCHED AS she got into the car and drove off with the stranger. If the storm hadn't been approaching, she would have stayed.

He was sure of it.

Bad timing.

That's what it was.

Or fate.

He stood up, the field of grass around him so tall she hadn't noticed him running toward her after she'd first pulled over.

Then he packed up his bag.

Maybe this was fate's way of letting him know he'd been reckless. That he shouldn't have abandoned his plan just because a tempting opportunity had come up.

Maybe it was time to go back to the drawing board altogether.

He sighed into the rain.

No matter the reason, there was no denying the eventual outcome.

Bella Greene was going to be his and nothing, and no one, was going to stop that.

Chapter One

Two weeks later and Marco Rossi was ending a hell of a day.

"Does this town ever have predictable weather?" he asked, peeling his rain-soaked boots off his feet while water collected on his desk chair beneath him.

His partner and desk mate opposite him, Carlos Park, wasn't faring much better. He mumbled when he spoke, trying his Boy Scout best to dry himself off with some paper towels the sheriff had tossed them on his way out.

"Don't act like your weather was miles different than ours. You came here from North Carolina, not Switzerland."

Marco couldn't fault that truth. Though he was, as his sister often said, a hothead. Which meant when everyone else was trying to stay cool, he was always at an even spicy. He was, after all, Italian. Born in New York to a family who could be traced back all the way to Sicily.

If they were still around, Marco was sure he'd be sitting somewhere near them now, still being just as spicy.

But a lot had changed since he was five, in New York and as part of that family.

A lot.

"Our wild-card weather was more light showers and the occasional ice storm," he returned. "Not chilly one second, monsoon the next."

Carlos shook out a sigh.

While Marco had been having a day of it, Carlos seemed to be having a week of it. They might have been partners but the Dawn County Sheriff's Department had been understaffed since The Flood, the name locals had given to a series of events that had shaken everyone's faith in the community.

It sounded dramatic because it was.

The extraordinary tale of corruption and crime within town leadership that led to murders and more, making state and national news and leaving a whole lot of mess in its wake.

A by-product of the mess?

Locals still not trusting anyone they didn't know.

Which was why Marco was having a bad day.

Carlos's bad luck, however, ran more personal.

"I just don't get it, man," he said, all exasperation. "She told me she had a great time and to give her a call if I wanted to do it again and *I did* and now she's a phantom."

That got Marco. He laughed.

"She *ghosted* you. She's not a phantom."

Carlos threw the wad of paper towels he'd collected onto his desk. It landed next to his tray of paperwork. Most of it was old. The interim sheriff and lead detective were trying their best to comb through old cases for one reason or the other. That meant that every deputy in the bullpen had a tray full of files, no matter how uneventful the month had been so far.

"Whatever it is, I'm not a fan," Carlos said. "I'm going to have to see what Millie thinks. Get a woman's opinion on what to do next."

Millie Dean was a name that had made the news less than a year before, along with that of her brother's. They'd gotten caught in the fallout of The Flood and, thanks in part to Dawn County's lead detective, Foster Lovett, they'd all survived it. Now Millie had an engagement ring on her finger and the total and utter appreciation and respect of Carlos. Something that, according to Libby at the front desk, wasn't easily earned.

Carlos pulled his phone out and tried to wipe it down with the already-wet paper towels. It made him grumble again.

"How about we go out for a drink instead?" Marco looked up at the clock on the wall. Their shift had technically ended half an hour ago but helping Mrs. Finnigan get her car looked at had taken longer than either expected, no thanks to the rain.

It had been an odd déjà vu for Marco to find another truck broken down on the side of the road. This time, instead of encountering a woman he still couldn't get out of his head with a wrench in one hand and deep mistrust in her eyes, they'd been met with a deflated tire and a woman hell-bent on letting them know just how much she hated the Auburn football team.

"You can give me some more fun facts about the town and I can pay you for it in free drinks," Marco added.

That seemed to do the trick. Carlos perked up.

"You had me at *free*."

Marco reached into his gym bag next to his desk and pulled out his tennis shoes. He laughed.

"That's the second to last thing I said," he pointed out.

Carlos waved him off.

"And it was the magic word. Now let's get out of here before another call about car trouble or weird power outages comes in." He started to stand but paused. "Let's also make sure I don't text Janice again. Not until after I talk to Millie first."

Marco gave him a thumbs-up. He liked Carlos but didn't know him all that well yet. Which meant he wasn't about to point out that his experience with the ladies only ever earned him the status of a short-lived Casanova. He knew how to do the one-night stands and serial-dating moves; he didn't have the experience in anything that was supposed to last.

Once again his sister, Amy, had an opinion on that too.

I think all kids who were given up for adoption have trust issues, Marco. That doesn't mean you have to drag them into your romantic life too.

It was an old piece of sisterly advice but she'd been doling it out more frequently since her marriage to her high school sweetheart. She'd found love and she wanted the same for him.

Instead she'd watched him transfer out of his job, their hometown and to a place in dire need of a second chance.

No one was perfect.

Marco changed into his gym clothes and met Carlos out at the only bar in Kelby Creek.

Once a motel, then renovated into a bed-and-breakfast and then split into a bar, storage and office spaces for rent, the Rosewater Bar was as eclectic as some of its regulars.

Marco had been there twice already and gave a polite nod to the local psychic as he went in. She was at a table with the neon pink–haired coroner, Amanda Alvarez. Carlos made a bee-line for the group while Marco went to the bar to order two beers.

It was almost six at night and his stomach growled as he waited. He started to wonder if Carlos wouldn't mind grabbing a bite to eat instead of a second beer when the front door to the bar opened and a new set of patrons walked in.

Bella Greene was nothing but magnificent.

Even in overalls.

Her hair was twisted up in a messy bun, though half of the light brown locks had escaped and rested against the denim straps across each shoulder like she'd meant to do it that way. However, Marco got the feeling it wasn't a deliberate style. Instead he picked up more of a Belle vibe from the woman, the heroine from *Beauty and the Beast*, a movie that Amy had had on repeat when she was in middle school. It was like Bella had been wandering around in her overalls, patches of dirt across the pants, and had only come into the bar because she was guided by someone.

Her eyes, ice blue, were still on her companion as he let the door shut behind them.

They were laughing.

Marco didn't like the man, though he knew how irrational that was.

Bella followed him to a booth against the wall and they settled just as Carlos made his way over to the bar. Marco averted his gaze from the woman he'd barely had a conversation with and looked at the defeat on his partner's face.

Marco snorted.

"Listen, I said I'd keep you from texting Janice. You never said anything about keeping you from talking to a psychic or medical examiner."

Carlos rolled his eyes and it was their turn to find a seat.

Marco still had a sightline to Bella but tried to keep his attention off her. Though he'd already failed that in the last two weeks. The ride from her truck to the restaurant had indeed been almost ten minutes on the dot. During that time their conversation had been limited to a few throwaway facts about their route into town, the mention that she worked with her brother and father, and that she'd been to North Carolina on vacation but hadn't been to where he'd moved from.

Then Marco had waited in the parking lot

until two men, dressed as fancy as she had been, had picked her up.

Because, while he fully understood how she could have thought his watchfulness was creepy, there had been something about the way she held herself that made his gut stand at attention.

Bella Greene hadn't just been wary of strangers, she'd been afraid.

Afraid and clutching a piece of paper.

Marco would have asked her about that detail had she still had it in her hand when she'd first gotten into the car, but she hadn't.

Still, it was enough to worry him.

Even after she'd left with, he assumed, her brother and father, Marco had wondered about the paper.

About her.

And now there she was across the bar from him. No fear, no note, no broken-down truck in the background while she held a wrench like a bat.

No—

Marco felt his brows push together seconds before the thought that troubled him was staring him in the face.

Carlos, who had been talking about how the attic above them had been part of some case, stopped midsentence.

"What is it?" he asked.

It might have been nothing but it might be something. Either way it wedged into Marco's mind like a popcorn kernel between teeth and he had to pick at it.

"How long have you been working at the sheriff's department?"

Carlos was fast with his math.

"Seven years and a few months. Why?"

"In that time, how many calls have you gotten for people with broken-down vehicles?"

This time he wasn't as fast.

"Uh, I mean, I can't really remember every one but I'd guess…twenty times? Maybe? Why? What are you thinking?"

Marco tapped his thumb against the beer bottle. He looked back over at Bella.

"I've been to four since I got here."

Carlos shrugged.

"Half of the town works outside Kelby Creek. Stands to reason that breakdowns would happen. Maybe since it's been colder than normal for us, people have been moving around more."

Marco nodded but that kernel was still there.

He decided not to mention that, of the four he'd responded to—Bella included and the first—every one of them had been a woman. Brunettes, to be specific.

Coincidence, Marco told himself.

He took a swig of his beer and forced himself back into the conversation Carlos had been trying to have.

Yet his mind and gaze kept wandering to the booth against the wall.

Bella.

And the paper that had been in her hand.

What exactly had it said?

BELLA HAD HAD an off day the first time she'd met Marco. She had known it then, knew it after when she replayed the meeting and knew it again when she finally realized he was in the same bar she was.

Not even the same bar, but standing at the edge of the booth and grinning.

She also had known and now knew again that Marco Rossi was a man whose image belonged on a poster in a teen girl's bedroom. Or a model in an ad that you saved to your phone and then sent it to your friends with fire emoji or GIFs of women fanning themselves.

Bottom line and with the bottom dollar, Marco was as good-looking as he had been weeks ago.

She, on the other hand, was no longer the woman who had threatened him with a rusted wrench while wearing her party heels.

Now Bella was in a familiar place, with a friend, and had already looked into Marco's tale of being a new deputy at the sheriff's department and deemed it true.

She was also now in, what her brother had dubbed, her yeehaw overalls. Something she wore on workdays when rain was predicted so she had enough pockets to store materials if it came down before she could find cover. Something that often happened despite all three Greenes having a radar app on their cell phones.

It wasn't a cute look, even without the dirt and mud splotches. At least now she wasn't terrified and ready to defend herself with whatever was around her.

It was the little things.

"Deputy Rossi!"

Marco laughed while she cringed. She'd overcompensated for her self-consciousness and applied her enthusiasm a little too hard. He was kind enough not to mention it.

"Miss Greene, nice to see you again."

The way his voice rumbled over her one-syllable name took the low heat from her drink and fanned it a little.

Justin, her current drinking buddy, wasn't as coy about it. His eyebrow rose in question. She hurried to answer it.

"Justin, this is the deputy I was telling you about. The one who gave me a ride when my truck broke down. Marco Rossi. And, Marco, this is my friend Justin Hastings."

Justin was his own kind of handsome, though it was more of a classic Hollywood type. He was tall, very tall, and wore suits that were custom, fitted and expensive. He had brown hair that was, as long as she'd known him, always cut short and impeccably groomed. Though she'd never thought it was polite to ask, she estimated his age to be midthirties. He'd become a local after Bella left town, and since she'd been back, he had been one of Greene Thumb and Hammer's biggest supporters. Like Bella he was good at networking *at* work but not the best at socializing outside of a small subset of people. Val and her father belonged to that group but were running behind because of the last rain.

"Nice to meet you," Justin said. "And thanks for helping Bella here out. I know her dad appreciated it since all of us were out of town."

They shook hands.

"It was no problem," Marco replied. "Just doing my job." He turned and addressed Bella directly. "Actually, if you don't mind, could I talk to you really quick? It'll take two seconds."

Color her surprised, Bella hadn't expected that. Justin, however, was the first to respond. He stood.

"I was just about to head to the restroom really quick so feel free to take my seat."

"Thanks, man."

Bella watched, confused and equally intrigued, as the deputy switched places with Justin.

"Sorry, I didn't mean to interrupt your date. I was just going to ask you something about your truck."

"It's not a date." Marco's brow rose, most likely at the quickness of the answer. It wasn't the first time someone had mistaken her occasional outing with Justin as more than platonic. "We're just friends. Justin and me, I mean. He's actually a client too."

For some reason, Bella felt she had to prove herself. She pulled out her phone and went to the second to last picture in her camera roll that she'd taken.

"See, we built a small shed for his mom when we first started the family business and he liked it so much that we're doing one for him now. It's bigger though, a sixteen-by-sixteen. We had to tarp what we had of it today because of the rain. Which is why I'm—well, wearing these."

Bella motioned to her outfit with one hand and used the other to hold the phone for him. He looked between the picture of the partially built shed and her overalls. It was around then that she realized she'd talked faster than normal.

She was self-conscious again.

Bella blamed it on the heat that was steadily crawling up her neck at his closeness. She had been caught wholly off guard by the man being in the bar. Never mind actually sitting across from her.

Her gaze went to his left hand. No ring and no tan line from one.

Did that mean he was single?

What if he was?

Bella could have kept entertaining those thoughts but then the man in question went and did it.

Deputy Rossi went and put his foot in it big-time.

Whether he meant it to be offensive or not, his next words threw whatever attraction she was feeling for the man out into the night.

"You actually did that? That's really impressive."

Maybe, just maybe, if he'd asked her father or brother that question instead, Bella wouldn't feel the anger pop up. But she'd already heard it and variations from several men throughout the last three years. None of them had been as good-looking as the deputy, but when it came to defending herself, nothing—including whether or not she wanted to run her hands through a man's hair—stopped her from standing tall.

Even if she was sitting down in a booth in a bar.

"Did I actually help build the shed I told you that I helped build?" she deadpanned. "Yeah. I did *actually* do that. You know, because it's my job."

She took her phone back with speed and went to her purse for a business card. She had it out and was handing it to him before he could find an appropriate response.

"See that name? Greene Thumb and Hammer, emphasis on the Greene part," she said, face going hot. "Not the Greene Men or Greene and Son. *All* of the Greene family." She decided it wasn't pertinent to amend her statement with the fact that her mother didn't help in any way with the business because she was happily and joyfully retired after years of working administration in a high school. Instead her arms went over her chest like armor.

Then the deputy finally rebutted.

"I didn't mean any disrespect." He also sat up taller. Going stiff like a football player ready to protect his quarterback. She'd offended him with her being offended. "I was just trying to say that it was impressive. I once tried to build a table for a girl I was dating and it fell apart."

Bella could feel part of herself cooling into regret. A part of her letting her know that she was, in fact, being a bit unreasonable. Yet she'd spent the last three years being questioned by enough sexist men to go for the throat before pulling back on the throttle.

"Oh, so because you can't do woodworking, then the fact that I, a woman, can do it is really impressive?"

"No. That's not what I meant either. I just didn't know what your job was. If you did the business or social media side or—"

Bella's eyebrow rose high.

He held up his hand to stop her.

"Wait. That sounded like I was proving your point, and I'm not," he interrupted. "You're taking this out of context. If you could just listen to me for a second and—"

"Oh, I *am* listening, *deputy*," she shot back. "I'm listening to every word."

Marco surprised her by making a strangled kind of grunting noise.

"What is it with this town and how much everyone talks?" he asked. "You're all so frustrating."

If she had mistaken his intent earlier, she knew she wasn't now.

"Frustrating? You just need to learn how to choose your words more carefully. We're living in the twenty-first century, Deputy. Not some kind of '80s cop movie where the short skirt with car trouble is only there for eye candy and a reason for the hero to want to save the day." Like Bella knew her anger was unreasonable, she knew part of it was from another place too. One of fear and worry.

One tied to a note she'd put in her bedroom safe.

But anger was unruly and it flailed around without hesitation and with no empathy for the man it was striking.

Bella went for her purse and pulled it up, readying to leave the table, the conversation and maybe the bar entirely.

Another man, however, changed her course.

Carlos Park, a longtime sheriff's deputy, which was a rare claim, considering what had happened to the department with The Flood, hustled up to the table, phone in hand.

He nodded to Bella, seemingly unaware that she was seething, but spoke to Marco.

"Sorry to interrupt but a call just came in that I'd like to check out. Mind if we go? I already paid the tab."

Marco's brows knitted together but he stood all the same. He glanced at Bella, nostrils flared.

There was that heat, that not entirely angry heat, again. Sizzling beneath the surface.

Bella doubled down on resisting it long

enough to make sure she didn't do the polite Southern thing and smile.

"That's no problem for me," Marco answered.

"No problem at all," Bella added. "It was good to see you again."

Just like that, Marco followed Carlos out into the night, leaving Bella to cool down from everything while Justin settled back into his original seat with a raised eyebrow.

It was only later that night, deep beneath her covers as she was trying to fall asleep, that Bella wondered what Marco had wanted to know about her truck.

And what situation he'd just run off to that had kept him from asking it.

Chapter Two

Sheriff Chamblin wasn't outside the local grocery store but Detective Lovett was. And boy, Marco hadn't spent a lot of time with him but could see he was spitting mad.

"A prank call," he grumbled, pocketing his phone into his off-duty clothes. He, Marco and Carlos were the only law who'd responded to Main Street and all three were in their street wear. The uniformed deputies had gone to the two other locations that had called in suspicious activities around town.

Apparently they hadn't found anything either.

Or, at least, not more than the two words spray-painted somewhere at their location.

Got you was small, in black spray paint and extremely annoying, staring Marco in the face from the brick wall on the grocery store's facade.

Detective Lovett ran a hand through his surprisingly long blond hair and stared at the words a moment. Then he blew out a breath.

"I get that this town has issues with us but I wish they'd funnel that into something else," he said. "Like running for local government and applying for the empty spots we have. Help us be the change we all want, not pull us in all different directions for a lousy prank."

"Small towns also breed boredom," Marco had to point out. "Doesn't mean whoever did this was trying to prove anything."

The detective agreed to that with a few small nods.

Then he was smiling apologetically at the men.

"Thanks for coming out. I know it wasn't a normal call but I had to reach out just in case."

It seemed Carlos, who had led the charge to Main Street, had lost the tension that had also wound Marco up without knowing why. They'd taken both of their cars and sped to Main Street with purpose and determination. Now those feelings ebbed into a tiredness for Marco. A low after an adrenaline high. He thought Carlos might be feeling the same. The deputy let out his own low, long breath, deflating his once-uptight stance.

He nodded toward the grocery store.

"The last time you came out to this place with

no plans on shopping, a lot went down," Carlos said. "I wanted to make sure that didn't happen again. At least not alone."

"And I'll be sure to let Millie know you two came to the rescue. Even if there was no rescue that was needed."

Marco knew what they were referring to— Millie and the detective had nearly died in the store when going up against a very angry and trigger-happy man—but neither man spoke to the story further.

Instead Lovett shook out his shoulders and cracked a grin.

"Since this isn't life or death and, since my lady is out with her ladies, what do y'all say about getting something to eat?" he asked. "Fallon and I usually eat together when Millie has a girls' night but he's out of town with his boyfriend and I really am not feeling the Hot Pockets I was eyeing in the freezer before the sheriff called me." The detective looked to Marco and added on, "Fallon is Millie's little brother. Really funny but can't cook to save his life."

"I'll take you up on that," Carlos was quick to say. "I've had half a beer and that only made me hungrier. Rossi?"

They both turned to Marco.

He wasn't a shy man by any means. In fact his sister, Amy, once likened him to a bottle rocket that kept going off. Hotheaded, loud and sometimes a spectacle.

But under the gaze of both men, Marco felt a wariness that often settled against his chest since his time at his last department in North Carolina.

Marco grinned but shook his head.

"Thanks for the offer but I think I'm going to head home," he said. "It's been a while since I got to bed early. I might try it tonight."

Both men accepted the answer and soon all were in their cars and off.

Marco's stomach growled as he drove and he didn't get into bed until one o'clock in the morning. He did, however, pull out the business card Bella had given him.

He'd met her twice now and both times she'd been different. The first she'd seemed worried, scared, ready to attack. The second? Ready to defend, quick to talk and wholeheartedly frustrating.

Marco had been told by his sister that he was quick to get under people's skin but he'd seemed to have broken a record with Bella Greene.

MONDAY WASN'T AS exciting as Friday had been but it did take a quick turn for interesting right after lunch. Of all people, Bella appeared next to his chair, brought in by their front desk clerk,

Libby. He hadn't expected to see Bella again but that didn't stop his body from reacting to her.

"Miss Greene," he greeted, trying his damnedest not to look her up and down. Still, it wasn't hard to notice she had gone from overalls to a worn set of blue jeans and a somewhat tight T-shirt that said Support Local on its front that looked just as good as the outfit from the night before. Her hair was partially down, the top framed by a red flannel hair band, and her lips were rimmed with gloss, the color of a peach, making her mouth as distracting as the freckles running across her nose and cheeks that he hadn't noticed in the darkness of an approaching storm or the low light of the bar.

"Deputy Rossi." Her tone was clipped. "I hope it's okay that I came by to see you."

Marco nodded to Libby that it was. He motioned to the chair butted up against his desk. He'd be a lying fool if he denied how aware he was of the lack of space between their knees when she sat.

"It's no problem. Though if we're about to go round two, I'd like to at least go make another cup of coffee first."

Bella snorted. A small smile tugged up the corner of her lips.

"That's actually one of the reasons I came by," she started. "I wanted to apologize for jumping the gun and somewhat accusing you of being sexist. See, when you work in a job like I do and hear some of the things I have, well, it makes you a little more defensive than normal. Hence the me-jumping-the-gun part."

That intrigued Marco. He felt his eyebrow rise in question.

"Jumping the gun implies that you jumped to a conclusion before you found out the facts. Which almost sounds like you still think I'm sexist, you just haven't found the proof yet."

That smile turned into a smirk fast.

"To be fair, I don't know you all that well," she countered. "Who's to say you aren't sexist and just waiting for someone like me to figure it out?"

Marco laughed.

"I guess I can't argue that airtight logic, now can I?"

"It must be *extremely* frustrating."

They kept each other's gaze as they stared in a silence.

Marco knew he should probably apologize but he'd never been too great at that. Instead he chose a different path.

He leaned back in his chair and let his smile melt down into a more professional expression.

"You said *one* of the reasons you came here? What was the other?"

Bella's sarcasm also changed. It turned into quick curiosity.

"I realized that I never got to answer your question the other night. The one about my truck? You never really got to ask it. So, I thought I'd try to see if I could answer it."

Marco hadn't forgotten but he had prioritized, their fight only making it easier. Work had shifted his wayward thought again and again until he'd apparently put it on a shelf. Now he got it back down.

"It's probably nothing but I was wondering what exactly ended up being wrong with your truck. I had a buddy in North Carolina who had a Tacoma and even the older ones tend to be more reliable than not."

It happened quick.

One second he was asking a simple question and the next everything went dark.

BELLA WAS THINKING about her truck. She was about to tell the deputy that, according to her former mechanic brother, it had been a problem with her fuel. That Val had cussed about the poor quality, suspecting it was watered-down gas.

She also started to feel the building sensation that she was going to have to pull her expression tight when she answered the question to keep it from slipping an inch and showing the man that what had happened that day had scared her. That the note written in its pristine handwriting and its three little words had put a wobble in her knees and a coldness in her gut.

That, even though weeks had passed and nothing else had happened, Bella still felt like the worst was yet to come.

And she'd been right.

Though she hadn't imagined it all would start at the sheriff's department.

Not when she was there.

Not when a part of her had started to relax on reflex being with the deputy.

The lights went out all at once, followed immediately by a pop sound.

Chatter kicked up around them. Someone close was asking about the backup generators when the darkness stayed thick. Bella's eyes were drawn to the light in the distance from the hallway's end that she'd just come through. There were no windows in the large room she was in now, since it was at the heart of the building, which only made every part of her go on the alert.

Bella's hands fisted into the thighs of her jeans. Adrenaline toggled her body between her fight-or-flight responses while her mind stuck to one sentence.

Hello there, friend.

Movement from her side jolted her to stand.

"It's probably another damn prank," someone on the other side of the room called out.

There were some answering grumbles while a flashlight app on a cell phone turned on near her. It illuminated enough of their area to show that Deputy Rossi's chair was empty.

Bella opened her mouth to say something but the lights came back on like they'd never had the audacity to go out.

Bella turned around to face the direction of the hallway she'd come through. She was startled by a figure looming between it and her.

Or perhaps protecting.

Marco was a wall of defense. Muscles visibly tensed, ready to strike. That tension lessened only as he faced her after a moment.

His brows slammed together but she couldn't place the emotion behind his new expression.

That made her uneasy.

Just like the memory of the note...and the box.

Bella had tried not to think of either but it was a rock rolling down a hill. Hard to stop once it started.

"I think that's probably all of the excitement I can take for my lunch break," she tried, adding on a smile she hoped wasn't strained. "I should get out of here while y'all see to what-ever happened."

Marco searched her face but nodded.

"I'll walk you out."

Bella accepted the escort and soon they were out in the somewhat cold air. October in South Alabama was always a mixed bag when it came to weather.

Even more so when it came to surprises.

Bella found another one as they stopped next to her truck.

This time, thankfully, it wasn't bad.

"You still don't know if you jumped the gun." Marco's words were strong and low. He had his hand on the opened driver's-side door of the truck.

"Beg your pardon?"

He half shrugged.

"About me," he clarified. "You drew some pretty harsh conclusions the other day—"

"Which I admitted I did without any real evidence," she added.

"Which you admitted but you still don't have enough now to know if you were right or not, do you?"

Bella moved her hand side to side to show she was on the fence. That heat, that slow burning that felt like they were doing more than just having an innocent conversation, started to move through her again.

Marco smiled. It was all polite.

"Then let me take you out to dinner tonight and redo my, I guess, second impression. Help you see if you jumped the gun about me."

Bella hadn't expected that. This time there was no hiding her thoughts.

Marco laughed, she assumed at her wary expression.

"Listen, I grew up in a small town and know that if you offend one local, you offend them all. Help me right that awkward wrong."

This time it was Bella who laughed.

"Fine," she agreed, hopping into the truck. When the door was shut, she rolled down the window. Marco hadn't moved an inch. He knew he had her attention. "But, let it be known, I'm paying for myself. Or will that be a problem, Deputy Rossi?"

Marco raised his hands in defense. His casual smile went into a smirk in a split second.

"Whatever rocks your boat, Miss Greene."

Chapter Three

"It's not a date."

Bella was at the top of a ladder, holding up one side of a rafter, and in a fight with her father and brother.

"This deputy man asked you out to dinner," her father repeated. "That sounds like a date to me."

It had been two hours since she'd come back from the sheriff's department. Bella should have kept her mouth shut about the experience but, when they were doing repetitive work like hanging rafters, chatting among themselves became a necessary habit to stay sane. That or listen to her father's alternative rock Pandora station for eight hours straight and, today, Bella wasn't feeling that.

"He's just trying to make up for putting his foot in his mouth and *I'm* trying to make up for getting so defensive way too quickly. It's not like there's another venue or activity to do those things. I'm not about to take him to the creek to fish and talk out our problems."

The scraping of a ladder's legs against the floor sounded as her dad moved to the rafter Val was holding, making sure it didn't fall out of the spot it had been wedged into. Their father was the most comfortable with heights and used the tallest ladder they had to move between each frame and temporarily screw it against the two-by-fours that ran along the top of each. It was the last thing they'd do as far as framing went before starting on building the walls.

It was also an extra pain for Bella but that was more from the fact that she was so short compared to the other two. The extra effort to reach the rafter she was supposed to be watching made her arms wobble even more.

It didn't help that, despite her experience doing what they were currently doing, she was still somewhat afraid of heights. That included their larger-scaled stepladders like the one she was currently on.

"I'm not even sure you should have dinner with him. You know nothing about him," her father went on.

Bella blew out a breath. The nip of cold she'd enjoyed earlier had melted into sweat at working.

"That's what the dinner is for, Dad. Getting to know him."

Her dad grumbled. It finally keyed in her brother, who had, weirdly, been quiet during most of the conversation. Though Bella expected that had more to do with the texts he was receiving and sending when he wasn't actively holding the rafter. If her father had seen his phone, Val would have received a talking to, she had no doubt.

"Wait, who is this guy again?" Val asked. "A deputy?"

She sighed.

"Like I said when I started the conversation, he's the sheriff's department's newest hire. He transferred from some small town in North Carolina."

"*To* Kelby Creek? Why would anyone want to do that?"

No one immediately responded but Bella knew it was expected of her.

"I don't know but, like I said, I don't know much about him. Which is why we're going to dinner."

Like all locals, their opinions about Kelby Creek had changed after what had happened with Annie McHale, who had been caught up in The Flood awfulness and the fallout from it. That went double for the sheriff's department.

Bella's father finished up with Val's rafter and

moved on to hers. He didn't speak again until the first screw was in.

"Maybe it's a good idea if you don't go to the department anymore, at least. There are still a lot of people angry in this town about how they failed us and, just because it starts with pranks, doesn't mean it will end with them."

Bella didn't know if Val or her father did it too, but she took a moment to glance up the hill to Justin's house. He wouldn't be back until his work ended at four o'clock.

His wife would never be back.

"At some point we had to expect the department to start rebuilding," she finally said. "Maybe Marco just wants to help do that."

"Or maybe it's the only place that will take him."

Bella found her brother's gaze. He shrugged.

"I'm just saying, you need to be careful, Bells. Not only with strangers but strangers with power in this town." He shook his head. "Especially since we've seen what our friends do with it."

No one, not even Bella, could dispute that. Though the urge to defend Deputy Rossi tickled the back of her throat.

She knew, logically, that not everyone should be held accountable for what had happened during The Flood but it was a hard feeling to shake.

The confusion, disbelief and betrayal.

Bella glanced back at the house in the distance.

She was grateful.

There were much worse things someone could feel.

SINCE MOVING BACK to Kelby Creek, Bella had lived in three different places. The first was in her old bedroom turned workroom at her parents' house. She'd had to rent a storage unit to hold her belongings and had spent three months sleeping on a daybed that her mother had bought to hang out with her dad while he worked. It hadn't been awful but it had been cramped. Especially when her dad continued working in there and her mother continued to hang out with him as he did it.

After being woken up at dawn on a Saturday by both, Bella had decided she needed a change.

That led to an alternative that wasn't that great but was a bit better. Bella had moved into her brother's guest bedroom in a house he'd bought to renovate with his ex-wife. Since the divorce happened two months into the process, most of the house was a total mess. The deal was that Bella could stay there rent-free as long as she helped him try to complete it.

That's where the idea of Greene Thumb and

Hammer had been born. She, Val and their dad framing walls and talking about how it wasn't all that bad to work together.

By the time the business got off the ground and they were getting good press, Bella had fallen in love with another house in need of attention. It was ten minutes from her parents' house and a mere ten houses down from her brother's house.

Two stories, two bedrooms and in desperate need of upgrading from its early '90s roots. Which included a hot water heater that was in desperate need of being replaced. It gave out more cold showers than warm and was wholly responsible for Bella being late to dinner, and it was why she was frowning when she took the seat opposite the deputy.

"I'm so sorry," she greeted. "I was holding out hope that my cold water would somehow go and stay hot and then somehow it was twenty minutes later and, well, it went all downhill from there."

Marco, who was giving absolute life to a black T-shirt, leather jacket and jeans, stood while she sat down. They were at Crisp's, where down-home cooking was the norm but fancy table settings were not. The only thing between them on the table was his drink and two plastic-covered menus.

"I hope you haven't been here too long," she added.

Marco waved her off.

"Don't worry. I was a little late myself because of work."

Bella pushed past Southern decency and instead was all curious.

"Did y'all find out what happened to the power? I heard someone when the lights were out say it was a prank."

Marco's jaw tightened, then unclenched. A flash of anger followed by calm.

Despite knowing her father and Val were overprotective of her, Bella decided then and there she needed to know why Deputy Rossi had come to Kelby Creek.

To help, to coast or a place to run away to?

"Someone messed with the building's outdoor breaker box and, prank or not, tampering with a state building like that is no small thing to do." It was a diplomatic answer. When he continued, his words, however, lost that official flare. "It's not the first *prank* I've dealt with since being in town. I knew the sheriff's department wasn't well-liked but I thought almost two years since all the trouble that's gone on before would have helped soften people's opinions, especially since it's a mostly new staff."

"You should know that small towns have long memories. That goes doubly for something like The Flood."

Marco's brow rose but he held off on whatever it was he was going to say. Their waitress, one of the actual owners of Crisp's, came up and took their orders. Bella didn't even have to look at the menu. She'd been getting Crisp's famous potato chip turkey sandwich since she was a teen. Not exactly gourmet, but absolutely delicious.

When the waitress was off with promises of a sweet tea showing up within the minute, Marco readjusted his focus.

His stare was as intense as it was stimulating.

Bella realized that while her mind wanted to answer the questions she had about the man across from her, her body didn't care.

It just liked being with the deputy.

THE FOOD WAS GOOD, the company was intriguing.

Marco finished off his burger and Bella finished telling her story about the time she and her father had dropped a bucket of paint down Val's house stairs and then tried to blame it on each other.

"What people don't get about dads is that they can get really sassy when they want to," she said, breaking a moment for another long pull of sweet tea. "Mine loves us, would take a bullet for us and won't hesitate to say he's proud of us and the business. *But* he'll also throw us under the bus to save his own skin." She snorted. There were no bad feelings in her tone. It was clear that the Greenes were a close bunch.

"What about you?" she added. "Any family back in North Carolina?"

Marco nodded.

"My parents moved to Chimney Rock, a small town outside Asheville, right after my sister, Amy, went with her husband back to New York. Though the way she talks about traffic and her commute to work, I'm thinking she'll come back to the South sooner rather than later."

A thoughtful expression crossed Bella's face. Marco had to give it to her, she definitely paid attention.

"*Back* to New York?" she asked. "Are you from there?"

Marco readjusted in his seat, putting his back a bit straighter in the chair. Though he felt fine with the subject, he'd come to dislike the reactions of pity or several questions that usually followed him talking about his family's past.

"My bio mother was." He dived in. "She died after Amy was born but my grandmother raised us in Queens until we had to go into foster care when we were five and six. We moved to North Carolina after our parents adopted us. They wanted to slow down and my mom is from there."

To her credit, Bella took the information in stride.

"I get the slowing-down thing," she said, skating over the parts that usually made people stumble. "I was working at a software company in Atlanta before I was laid off and came here. I missed the city rhythm at first but I find myself continuing to settle in more here. Though the pace hasn't exactly been slow in Kelby Creek since I got back."

She looked uncomfortable. Physically uncomfortable at the thought.

One that seemed to be easy for all the residents of Kelby Creek to get to without much prodding.

Marco didn't like the change. Just as he hadn't liked the look on Bella's face in the department after the power went out or in the parking lot.

It was one reason he'd been prompted to ask her to dinner.

One of several reasons.

Now he wanted to focus on the uncomfortable expression. The memory of something bad that had happened.

The Flood as told by a local outside of law enforcement.

"Feel free to not answer but, I'm sorry, I have to ask—" Marco made sure his voice was low enough so the patrons around them didn't hear but Bella still could "—The Flood... Was it as bad as the news said it was?"

Bella took her time answering, as if she were trying to find the perfect response.

"My brother, Val, used to be married to a woman named Darla," she started. "They were in love kind of like what you'd see in a romantic comedy. Goofy meet-cute at the grocery store, first date on the golf course with a late-night picnic that ended after the sprinklers came on, and that almost ridiculous kind of happiness that others can feel just by being in the same room with them." She'd smiled at the beginning and now that smile fell the more she spoke. "Everyone was surprised when Darla up and left Val, saying that she wasn't happy with him anymore and instead wanted to start a life with a guy she'd met in Mobile. But not as surprised as Val was. He told me that he didn't understand how someone he thought he'd known and loved for years turned out to be someone he didn't really know at all. But, even more than being upset at her for leaving, he'd been furious at himself for not seeing the signs. For not figuring out she'd been lying to him."

Bella's expression softened, as did her tone.

"When The Flood happened, we all became Vals. The people we'd grown up with, learned to trust and respect, hurt us, and worse, made a lot of us angry with ourselves. Angry that we never saw it coming."

"And I guess to make an entire town feel that way, it had to be bad."

Bella nodded and laughed, despite the topic.

"Yeah, I guess I could have just said that instead." She moved her straw around her glass, an idle motion that matched a faraway look that took over. "I think it'll be a long time before anyone around here lets go of what happened. Some people got far worse than being angry."

The waitress brought their check and pulled them out of their darkening conversation. Marco wanted to ask more specific questions but decided against keeping the dark topic going. True to her word, Bella paid for her meal and soon they were out standing between her truck and his Charger.

"You know, my dad also wanted me to find out why *you* came to Kelby Creek," she said around a smile. "He and my brother are really protective of me like that, which can be annoying." She took a step closer to him, leaving a foot or so of space between them. Marco got a better scent of the perfume he'd been smelling all throughout the meal. It smelled like cookies and Christmas.

"But, you know what? I don't think you're the kind of man who wants to admit that kind of truth." She tapped her chest with her index finger. "You're one of those guarded type of people, aren't you? The ones who wear invisible armor around their hearts."

Marco laughed.

"What are you, a mystical figure from an '80s fantasy movie?"

Bella rolled her eyes. It was in good humor.

"That would probably be a yes," she said with a nod. "I bet you have just as many secrets as charming smiles."

The lack of distance between them became charged. Somehow Bella had dipped, dodged and woven through his past, his present and now was throwing him off his game for the future.

Disarming was the word.

Bella Greene was distracting.

Marco took a small step forward. His gaze went to her lips before he had to drag it up to her eyes. Their height difference forced her head back, drawing attention to how bare and perfect the curve of her neck was.

He smiled and lowered his voice when he spoke.

"Miss Greene, does that mean you think I'm charming?"

Bella's cheeks became flushed. For a second he wasn't sure she was going to respond but then she was the one with the smile.

"I said your smiles are. As for you, I haven't decided yet."

She took several steps back and only broke eye contact when unlocking her truck's doors.

Marco had to take a quick breath to steady himself. Or, rather, his body. He'd thought he had been quick to get underneath Bella's skin but, now, he realized it might have been the other way around.

"Thank you for dinner, Deputy," Bella said as she climbed into the cab of her truck. "Maybe we can do this again."

Marco opened his mouth with every intention of pointing out they didn't have to let the current night end, but what he actually said was much less obvious.

"Maybe next time I'll leave my armor off," he teased.

Bella took the comment and threw it right back.

"I don't think you're the kind of person that leaves his armor at home."

Another quick smile and Bella was off.

Marco got into his car but paused, his hand and the key hovering over the ignition.

He was so wrapped up in Bella, wondering if he was running from something, that he didn't notice the power go off in the restaurant behind him.

Chapter Four

The call came in on Tuesday night, just after Marco's shift ended. He was on his way to the parking lot when Carlos swooped in and asked if he'd give him a ride since his car was in the shop.

Marco obliged but didn't understand why Carlos wanted to respond to a call when two other deputies already had. It wasn't until he saw the way Carlos was staring at the woman who had made the call that Marco started to understand.

Deputy Park might have been trying his hand at dating but it was clear that Jennifer Parkridge had a special place in his heart. A place that had woken up at the news that her house had been broken into. Off duty or not, that was enough to get the man over to the scene.

If the responding deputies minded the second set of questions, they didn't say so. Once they had confirmed no one was still in the house or in the area, they'd separated and spread out, along with Detective Lovett, who *was* on shift.

Jennifer was clearly shaken but, thankfully, okay. She hadn't been home when the break-in happened.

"I was out with Madeline going over some figures on a work project and only came by to grab a few files before heading back out," Jennifer explained to them once everyone had left. "I didn't notice the broken planter or the back door being busted until I was about to leave again."

She walked them into the house and to the back door. Sure enough, it looked like it had taken a powerful hit. The wood around the lock was splintered, all the way down the doorframe too.

"How do I even fix this this late?" Jennifer asked, palpable fear thumping against every syllable. "I can't just leave it like this."

Carlos was quick to answer.

"You don't worry about it. We can fix this tonight," he offered, slapping back at Marco, "Right?"

Marco was still focusing on the house. He heard their conversation but his attention was splitting. He nodded, then immediately regretted it.

"See? Don't worry, Jen. We can get this all squared away. You just worry about work."

Jennifer let out a sigh that held more stress than any one person should. Her smile was tired but seemed genuine enough.

"Thanks, Carlos," she said. "I'll be attached to my phone all night. Call me with anything."

Carlos saw her out, helping with the boxes she'd come home for, and then was back looking as close to sheepish as Marco had seen his new partner.

"She works at a lawyer's office in the city."

"And she left you and a stranger in her house while she went back to it?" That seemed a little more friendly than stereotypical small-town community trust. Especially considering Kelby Creek was a small town that had lost that trust, doubly so for the sheriff's department.

"We, uh, go way back." Carlos cleared his throat and then seemed to decide against a more diplomatic answer. "She was engaged to my older brother for a while during college. It didn't work out because he's a horndog. But if you ask me, he never deserved her."

Carlos's gaze trailed to the front window where the headlights of Jennifer's car flashed by as she pulled out into the street.

Marco liked Carlos but, when it came to personal lives, he had already decided not to make the same mistake he'd made in his old depart-

ment. Friendships there had only created problems when the incident happened.

The same one that had caused him to transfer
to Kelby Creek in the first place.

He wasn't ready to chance something like that
happening again, so Marco steered clear of any
personal talk and motioned to where Jennifer
had found the shattered planter just inside her
living room archway.

"So the door and the planter were the only
things that were damaged?"

Carlos zipped back to attention.

"Yeah. I'm guessing whoever broke in was
keeping the lights out or just using a flashlight.
Probably accidentally hit it since it was kind of
tucked out of the way."

Marco went through the motions of walking
through the hallway and living room. He passed
the flat-screen TV, a computer in the corner on a
desk beneath the window and went in the open
bedroom door, right up to a vanity covered in
loosely strewn jewelry. Carlos followed.

"And Jennifer said nothing seemed to be
missing."

Carlos nodded an extra affirmation.

"She did a walk-through with Foster to make
sure."

"But why? Why go through the trouble of
breaking into someone's house, only to leave

without doing anything? I can get not wanting to steal the bulkier items but why not grab the easier stuff?"

Carlos shrugged.

"Maybe they chickened out? Got spooked by a car driving past or a neighbor moving around. Decided to cut their losses just in case."

Marco had that feeling again. That there was more, that something was off, but sidestepped them to the present.

"Regardless of the reasoning, there's a door we need to fix and I don't exactly know how to do that. Do you?"

Carlos stood tall.

"Nope, but I know how to search tutorials on YouTube!"

But right after they watched a few minutes of a tutorial online on how to repair a busted door and doorframe, Marco realized there was only one path to fixing both that night.

"Let me make a call," he told Carlos after they both admitted neither had the right tools for the job.

But Marco knew who might.

He dialed the number and stood on the front porch, already grinning when a woman's hurried voice answered the call.

"Greene Thumb and Hammer, this is Bella Greene, how may I help you?"

SHE HADN'T EXPECTED to talk to Marco so soon. In fact, Bella had been convinced that her talk of armor around his heart had been enough to squash whatever interest he might have had in her.

Not that she'd blame him. Bella hadn't known where that kind of talk had come from, yet there she had been with a man she barely knew, teasing him about not opening up.

To her.

To someone he barely knew.

Bella had sank into her couch when she'd gotten home from Crisp's. A full stomach and a full-body cringe.

She'd tried to keep her expectations low for the dinner and yet, there she had been, enjoying herself.

It was only after the meal had ended that Bella realized while she'd talked about herself and the town, somehow the topic of Marco's life had gone unchecked.

Well, until he'd told her he was adopted and had a sister.

Bella had rolled over on the couch, trying not to wonder about the life Marco had been living that had led him to Kelby Creek. She had grumbled into the throw pillow and found that not one part of her wanted to think about anything other than the man. It had been frustrating because, while she regretted telling Marco that he had armor, she stood by the observation.

It was one thing to drop the ball socially like Bella had since coming home; it was another to outright keep out all attempts at connection.

So when the call came the next night and Marco was on the other end of it, Bella had to ask him twice to repeat his name. Though it wasn't like he had called her for a second outing.

He'd called her because of a broken door.

"This is just a shame," Bella's dad said from the passenger seat. He'd been tsking off and on since Bella had relayed the call to him and Val. Her brother only a few grumbles off.

"You know, I think this is an eye-opener for us," he said from the back seat. "We need a security camera at the office. One of those fancy ones that we can record and open on our phones."

Bella pulled up behind the red Charger, and her stomach started to flutter in anticipation. That flutter only became more aggressive as Marco himself stepped out onto the front porch.

Bella made sure not to give an inch to her family and stayed on the topic at hand.

"Our offices include a room in Dad's house,

your truck bed when the weather permits and a square of my kitchen counter," she pointed out. "Plus, it's not like we have anything valuable just lying around. I'm still not convinced that you don't sleep in the same room with your favorite electric saw."

Val made a noise like a snort.

"For how much we paid for that thing, you'd sleep with it too," he mocked.

"All right, let's focus," their dad said as Bella cut the engine. "I want this to be right so Jennifer doesn't have to add a busted door to her list of worries. Val, grab the tools. Bells, since you know these guys, you're stuck with being the nice person."

Bella groaned and Val laughed. Being the nice person was code for being a buffer between a client and the work they were currently doing. Depending on the site, the job and the client, it switched between the three of them. Though, as Bella had been sure to point out regularly, that hardly ever included their father.

They jumped out into the night air and started to pull materials from the truck bed. Marco began to walk down the driveway to them.

"Wait, I thought it was Carlos Park that called," Val whispered. "Who's this guy?"

Her father, ever the well-humored, was less quiet with his answer.

"That's the guy Bella went on a non-date date with."

"What?" Val returned.

"Dad, stop it," Bella said at the same time.

Marco, unaware, made it to the truck.

"Hey, guys, thanks for coming out."

Just like the call had been a surprise, the way he greeted them was different from what she had expected. It wasn't matter-of-fact or brooding. He was all smiles and extended handshakes. Something she knew was a slam dunk when it came to meeting her father for the first time.

"No problem," she said. "We're more than happy to help."

They did a quick round of introductions and then got down to business. Carlos showed them to the door and planted himself next to it, arms crossed and clearly determined to watch. Bella's dad gave her a nod that let her know it was okay not to try and nice-person him away. After she helped set up the tools, she moved back to the living room, where Marco had stationed himself.

At first he didn't seem to notice her presence. Even in profile, he looked like he was mulling something over. She probably could have assisted the repair and Marco would have been fine.

Bella cleared her throat.

"So, I talked it over with Dad and Val, and we're not going to charge anything for this job."

Marco turned to her but he still seemed far away.

"You might have to fight Carlos on that. He seemed really determined to pay for it."

Bella shrugged.

"It's not that big of a job. It would actually be preferable to doing any extra paperwork. Val usually does that and he complains the entire way through. Not getting paid would *be* payment enough."

Marco nodded to that. His gaze listed over to a wooden stand next to the doorway.

"Why would you break into someone's house but not take anything?"

His voice had hardened. Gone colder. Like it had detached from knowing the person it was with. Bella followed his gaze back to the wooden stand.

"Uh, did I do something instead?"

"Do something?"

"Yeah, I mean, if I didn't take anything, do I do something to something? Like rearrange the furniture or shred important documents?"

"Shred important documents?" Marco's eyebrow slid up. He grinned.

"Hey, I've seen enough TV shows and movies to know that sometimes people break into places with the sole purpose of shredding sensitive papers," she said. "Or scan them! I forgot about scanning them."

Marco turned his head away from her, looking in the direction of where the bedrooms must be. He shook his head and returned to the conversation.

"I'm pretty sure she doesn't have a scanner here and that nothing else happened." Marco let out a breath.

"And it wasn't another prank?"

He crossed his arms over his chest. That tone came back.

"If this was a prank, then whoever is behind them is escalating," he said. "And following a weird trajectory. Flipping the breaker at a sheriff's department and then breaking into a house only to do nothing and leave."

"Maybe it's who's getting targeted that's important? Law enforcement and then a lawyer? Doesn't Jennifer still practice law? I know she did when she helped with Val's divorce."

He didn't light up but Marco did seem intrigued.

"Could be."

They stood in silence for a moment, both looking at the room. Bella felt the urge to talk about armor again but decided to think of something else.

"To see if I could." The words came out before she could structure them correctly.

Marco's eyebrow slid up again in question.

"Bella? Come here a sec!" Val's voice broke in before she could answer. "Or, actually, go to the truck and grab my flashlight. Dad's is out."

"On it," she yelled back. Then, to clarify her thought, Bella turned to the deputy. "Even if you break in to someone's house and don't take anything, you've already done something by breaking in in the first place. That's the only other reason I think I'd do it."

"Break in just to see if you could," he added.

Bella nodded.

Then she was back out in the night air.

Marco didn't follow. She tried not to be disappointed.

Chapter Five

The house was quiet and cold. Bella dropped her keys on the entry table and didn't even care that she missed the flamingo dish they always went in that her mother had given her for Christmas. She was distracted and there was no point in pretending that it was by anyone other than a tall, dark and handsome deputy.

She knew Kelby Creek was a small town but that didn't keep her from noting how she seemed to be drawn to the man. That, whether intentionally or not, they kept bumping into each other.

Bella sighed into the mostly dark house. A month ago, her thoughts hadn't been this frustrating.

She went to her bathroom at the back of the home and decided that her plan of watching late-night HGTV to unwind would have to wait. Greene Thumb and Hammer had had a long workday. The chance of rain for the next three days waffled between 60 and 80 percent. That meant that the big sheets of plastic she detested had to come out. She and Val had rotated between three different ladders to cover Justin's custom shed-in-progress while her father had used clamps to hold it in place.

Because perfect first attempts were seldom, they'd had to readjust a few times.

Then there had been the trek up the sloped backyard to Justin's house. It was a large plantation-style home with two-story columns along the front porch and balcony, white siding and black shutters framing windows he'd had to replace, considering the age. It was one of a kind in Kelby Creek and had been a purchase he'd made with his wife with the intention of renovating, modernizing and then selling it.

But then The Flood had happened and Justin's plans had seemingly died along with his wife.

Now, almost two years later, he was paying them good money to make a custom shed for all the things he didn't want to keep in his garage.

Which, if Bella were being honest, never made much sense to her. He had plenty of space in his garage as it was. He was even letting them store their tools there overnight for safety. Why did he need another place for tools?

"It's a guy thing," Val had said once when she asked him and their father the same question. "When it comes to storage, more is better."

Either way it was a pain to pull their cart up the slope and that had been before one of the tires had popped and they'd had to transfer each tool individually by hand.

Honestly, it was nothing too bad in the grand scale of things but each task had really rubbed her the wrong way today. Bella had been thoroughly annoyed as she went home and was still feeling it when someone had called the work landline.

When that person turned out to be Marco, well, that had changed her minor stress to a different kind of tension. One that she needed to unwind from now.

She turned the shower faucet to hot and went into her bedroom to undress. Since she was no longer living with her brother, Bella had reverted to blasting music while she showered. Tonight she put on an '80s station from her Pandora app and made sure to grab a fresh towel from the pile on the chair in her bedroom that she'd been meaning to fold and put away for a week.

"Hungry like the Wolf" filled the bathroom, mingling with the building steam. She thanked God for the hot water and stepped in. Bella sang the lyrics to the song, only one of four she knew by heart, while she showered. It was a nice way to forget about everything else for a while. An easy way.

She was almost sad she had to get out and go to bed, knowing that if she didn't instantly fall asleep, her thoughts would revolve around a man she barely knew, but if it didn't rain the next day, then work would be tiring. She needed her rest, and kept that mini pep talk on repeat in her head as she got out and wrapped the towel around her.

It was a good talk with a good reminder.

But then she looked at the mirror and every part of her froze in place.

The music faded around her, the invading cold from no longer being wrapped in heat hitting her wet skin dulled. Her breathing caught and shallowed.

The only thing that sped up was the beating of her heart.

Bella's eyes were locked on the mirror.

Or, rather, the words written in condensation across its surface.

She saw the fear in her own eyes as she re-read the three words.

Hello there, friend.

MARCO DECIDED TO take a run that night. Jennifer Parkridge's back door was shut and locked, Greene Thumb and Hammer had left their card behind if she had any questions and Carlos had given Jennifer the all clear.

Detective Lovett had called him around the time they were getting ready to leave Jennifer's and Marco hadn't stayed long enough to eavesdrop.

He was restless when he got to his apartment and that restlessness had turned into the decision to run.

Though that decision wasn't exactly a fruitful one.

Each step against the asphalt, each kick up of rock and dirt, each pulse of endorphins only pushed him deeper into a sense of urgency. Of concern.

An itch he couldn't scratch.

Instead of continuing to try to figure it out, he decided around the third mile, according to his smartwatch, to redirect his focus on his surroundings. Without wanting to or meaning to, he compared them to North Carolina.

Which led him right to thinking about the sheriff's department he had once sworn he'd never leave.

You don't have to go, Rossi. You're blowing this entire thing out of proportion.

No matter how many days passed since he'd heard those words and no matter how far away he got, Marco still felt a deep anger well up inside him.

Trying to do the right thing wasn't always easy but he couldn't help resenting how hard it had been all the same.

Kelby Creek wasn't the only one with trust issues.

The chill in the air from the day had dropped down into actual cold. Marco wasn't a marathoner when it came to running but he did enough work that he made sure to never be caught in the South outside in anything more than a tank top and shorts. Now both were starting to retain sweat. He decided to slow down and turn back so he wouldn't be miserable on the way home if he kept up with what was turning out to be a long, long run.

Marco's apartment was just outside a neighborhood that looked like a mini suburb in the city. Houses were close together and bathed in the light from occasional streetlamps. Front lawns held lawn ornaments, kids' toys or some variation of the two. There were a few houses that needed a face-lift but most seemed well-kept and loved.

He ran by one that had an industrial dumpster in the driveway, most likely for ongoing construction on the inside, and wondered what kind of home Bella lived in. During their dinner, the most he'd said about where he lived was the name of the apartment complex, if she knew it, and then complained slightly about his second-floor neighbors who were a little too in love. Since she worked in construction, did she prefer a ready-to-move-in home or had she gone with a fixer-upper because she didn't mind the hassle of making a house her own?

Marco could have asked her those questions, or any for that matter, while they waited for her father and brother to do the repair. Instead they'd stayed relatively quiet. Maybe the armor comment wasn't too far off.

Or maybe it was that urgency, that restlessness, that had him off his game.

How could he focus when he was sure there was *something* going on and he was all but missing it?

You need to get out of your own head, he mentally chided himself. *Not everything ends up being a case.*

He nodded into the night to reaffirm the belief and took a right turn out of the neighborhood. Most of Kelby Creek had some kind of view of woods and the road that led from this neighborhood to the apartments was no exception. There were tree lines on either side of the street and very little light that carried in between them. It was why Marco had a pocket flashlight hanging by a cord on a wrist and his phone tucked into the waistband of his shorts.

It was also why he should have seen the car coming sooner.

Much sooner.

But he didn't. The best Marco could do was lunge to the side as the car appeared.

He yelled out in pain as something struck his hip. The force of it pushed his center of gravity off. Marco hit the dirt shoulder hard.

There was no time to assess the damage.

He whipped his head up to see the car slam on its brakes a few yards away.

Marco couldn't make out too many details but he could see enough to make his gut worry that it wasn't an accident. There was no license plate, for one.

For two? When the driver stepped out of the car, he made no move to run over and check on the man he'd just struck.

Instead he turned around slowly, just inside the driver's-side door.

It turned out that Marco's gut had been right to worry.

The driver was wearing an oversize black coat, dark pants and gloves.

But the most concerning part was the mask, and not just any mask.

It was the Ghostface mask from the movie

franchise *Scream*. A white face stretched to have wide black eyes and a mouth that sagged while black cloth wrapped around and behind the head, hiding any distinguishable features.

Marco held on to the hope that it was someone getting ready for Halloween a few weeks away.

"Hey," Marco called out. "Dawn County Sheriff's Department! Step away from the vehicle!"

The man didn't move.

Marco struggled to stand. The pain at his hip was radiating. The full car itself couldn't have struck him or he'd have been much worse off. He bet it was the passenger-side mirror that had clipped him.

Even though he was pretty sure the driver had meant to collide with him head-on.

"I'm a deputy with the sheriff's department and I'm telling you to step away from your vehicle," Marco yelled out again. He went for his phone but it wasn't there. He didn't want to take his eyes off the man to look for it either.

Since he was on a run, he hadn't thought to bring his service weapon or his badge.

He regretted both decisions.

The man shook his head.

Adrenaline was already moving through him, now the floodgates had opened.

Everything happened too fast.

The man got back into the car. Marco started to run at it, hoping to stop him before he could drive away. It was a fool's errand. His hip was killing him. It made for a labored limping gait.

There was still several feet between them when the reverse taillights came on.

Marco knew he only had two choices.

Stand his ground and hope the driver was bluffing, or try his best to make it into the trees before he found out the man wasn't.

Though, in hindsight, that wasn't much of a choice at all.

HE SHOULDN'T HAVE done it. He knew that. He *knew* that.

But he had. He'd done it anyway. He'd left his plan and become impulsive. Become reckless.

Become angry.

Which was bad.

So bad it could ruin everything.

"You're smarter than this," he told the basement. "You shouldn't have done that."

The basement didn't answer. There was no one in it besides him, but that wouldn't be the case for long. He looked at the suitcases, empty but ready, in the corner. His eyes lifted over to the chair, the ropes and the syringes he was hoping he wouldn't have to use.

Then it was Bella.

The pictures of her pinned to the corkboard didn't do her justice. Nothing did. Only her. Only *being* with her.

He walked up to his favorite picture and traced her lips with his thumb.

She was lovely.

They would miss her.

They would try to stop him—try to stop fate—to keep her.

"But I'm not going to let them," he said.

Anger pulsed through his resolve. Anger at an obstacle he hadn't foreseen.

Deputy Marco Rossi.

He growled at just thinking the name.

He wasn't good for the plan. For her.

Which was why the plan was changing yet again.

Instead of taking his time, things were about to get a lot more chaotic.

In fact they already had.

He looked down at the mask in his other hand.

Then he smiled.

Chapter Six

"This is ridiculous."

Marco opened the to-go box in the small hospital room. Carlos shook his head, pointed to its contents and decided he was funny.

"No. That's pancakes." He sat in the chair by the bed.

Marco rolled his eyes and caught the plastic cutlery that came along with his surprise meal. He knew he looked rough without seeing the quick frown on his partner's face. He'd gotten painkillers for the worst of it, despite trying to persuade the doctor that he was fine. Marco was glad now that he hadn't listened.

"I meant having to wait to be discharged," Marco clarified. "I'm good now and just want to get home and change and get back out there. Not stay holed up here."

He motioned to the hospital room around them.

Haven Hospital was Kelby Creek's only healthcare facility of any size. Privately funded, it was small, clean and surprisingly modern. That still didn't make Marco feel good about being there though. He'd only agreed to be admitted in the first place because the amount of blood along his side had been alarming.

Well, and the fact that the sheriff himself had ordered him to go.

Now, hours after escaping into the woods and walking back to his apartment, he *was* fine. Bruised, stiff and sore, but fine. No broken bones, no internal bleeding, no concussion.

Carlos, however, wasn't as convinced. He moved to Marco's side.

"Even if you were discharged, you wouldn't be back out there today. You were hit by a car and then had to anger your injury by walking a few miles before you got help. And, unless you've squeezed in a quick nap since, I don't think you've slept yet. If the doctor didn't make sure you were good before clearing you, he wouldn't be doing his job. Wouldn't you do the same in his place?"

Marco grumbled. Carlos wasn't wrong.

It still didn't mean he liked being told to stay in a hospital bed. And in a hospital gown to boot. He'd already been eyeing his bag of clothes that he'd grabbed before coming to Haven, sitting on the love seat along the wall.

If he thought he could get away with changing into them, he definitely would have already.

"Now, since I think your rumbling means you know I'm right, why don't you eat your breakfast? Not eating delicious pancakes won't change the fact that you have to wait it out. It's just you punishing yourself."

"Fine," Marco relented. "I'll eat the pancakes. But if I'm not out of here in an hour, I'm leaving. Even if that means escaping through the window."

Carlos eyed the third-story window but didn't point out the pitfalls to that plan. Instead he stood and readjusted his holster. He was on duty, just like Marco was supposed to be.

"We're going to find whoever did this," Carlos said after a moment, all humor gone. "It's one thing for this town to have trust issues. It's another to do this."

He didn't stay long after that, but he did make sure that Marco had his number written down since his contacts list was now gone. After he'd borrowed a neighbor's phone in the apartment complex, deputies and the sheriff alike had swarmed the area where he'd been struck. No one had found his cell.

Which was extremely annoying.

No one wanted to deal with replacement phones when they were trying to find the son of a bitch who tried to kill them. At least, not Marco Rossi.

He leaned back against the bed for a few minutes and wallowed in frustration until his stomach growled. The smell of the pancakes lured out his practical side. If he couldn't control anything else, he'd at least control filling his belly.

He was two bites into his new plan when a knock sounded on the door. Other than Carlos, only the sheriff had visited when he'd first come in. Maybe he'd returned because they found something? Or maybe Carlos had a change of heart and was going to help him break out.

"Come in."

Ice blue.

Marco found her eyes first and then the rest of the details filtered in. Her hair, almost the color of honey, was pulled up in another messy bun, strands hanging down to frame a face where freckles danced cheek to cheek and lips that he'd seen colored peach the night before were turned down in a severe line.

Bella was only timid for a moment. Long enough to look him up and down. How he wished he wasn't sitting up in a hospital bed, wearing a gown partially covered by a blanket and eating pancakes over a tray.

For whatever reason, he didn't want her to

see him like that. To be down and out. It was bad enough Carlos and the sheriff had seen that.

"I heard you got hurt," she started, leaving her spot by the door and stopping next to the bed. Marco noted her eyes were also a little bloodshot, like she was tired. Or maybe had been crying? Surely not about him. "Libby said it was a hit-and-run?"

"I forgot how fast news travels in a small town." He smirked, trying to lighten the mood, but Bella didn't seem to accept the change. He sighed. "I was out on a night run because I couldn't sleep and the next thing I know some guy hits me." He motioned to his side, hidden under the blanket. "I was lucky he wasn't going that fast when it happened. I'm bruised and the cuts were only superficial wounds. I'm fine."

Those cold blues seemed to scan him again, as if the quick pass could prove him true or false. He expected more questions or maybe even a quick verbal barrage telling him of the dangers of running so late, but as usual Bella Greene caught him off guard.

"I only know what happened because I came to the department this morning, hoping to catch you when your shift started." Her voice hollowed a bit toward the end. Like she was walking on eggshells over her own words. Marco moved to sit up straighter, finally feeling the tension in the woman, but winced.

It was a move that Bella didn't miss.

Worry contorted her expression.

"I—I shouldn't be here," she hurried. "I thought about waiting? Or calling up here? But then I started thinking about how you're new to town and you might not have anyone to check on you yet or that maybe your family was still in transit so you might need a friend. And *then* I thought I could tell you in person because surely I'd sound crazy on the phone but—"

She had her keys between her hands, fiddling with them. Marco grabbed all three to steady her.

"I appreciate you coming," he interrupted, though he left out the part where he hadn't told his parents or sister what had happened. That would be a call he'd make after he got a phone again and not one he made through the hospital. "It was really thoughtful of you, and nice."

Bella nodded but she didn't return his smile.

Something was off with her.

And he didn't like it.

Marco let go of her hands and leveled his gaze.

"Now, what did you want to tell me?"

"My roommate in college, Darcy, had a really bad breakup right before spring break our sophomore year." Marco didn't stop her seemingly odd jump in topic. Instead he listened, focused. "She went to one of her sorority's parties to try to distract herself but, instead, found a lot of hunch punch. A sorority sister called me because Darcy ended up locking herself in a closet and talking about how she wasn't ever coming out. *So* I walked into this room filled with mostly tipsy ladies all trying to coax Darcy out and did the first thing that came to mind to try to help. I bent down, put my face against the door and said, *Hello there, friend.*" Bella would have smiled at the story had the purpose of it not chilled her to the bones now. Still, she paused where the smile would have gone. Marco was patient and waited through it.

"It was just the first thing that popped into my mind but it weirdly did the trick," she continued. "Darcy came out and her sisters thought it was so funny that they started greeting me like that. All over campus, at every event, until eventually I even started saying it after college, at my old job and when I moved back. It just became my thing."

Bella's palms were sweating. Not because she was nervous to tell Marco what she was about to tell him, but because she couldn't help but see the words in her head, written in an email, a note, a box and now a mirror in her home.

It wasn't just terrifying.

It was violating.

She sat down on the edge of the bed, so close she would have been distracted by that closeness otherwise, but instead she went to her purse. The paper felt worn in her hand as she pulled it out. Bella handed it over and let him unfold it.

"Hello there, friend," he read.

Bella shifted in her spot.

"The day I met you, when my truck was broken down, I found that in my tool bag."

Marco flipped the paper over, ran his hand across it and flipped it back over.

Then he was all eyes on her again.

Bella knew by his look that he'd already figured out that part that made her feel like she needed to take another shower.

"And this isn't the first time you've gotten something like this," he guessed.

Bella shook her head.

"No. It's not." She took a deep breath and tapped the paper. "About six months before I found this, I got an email from some spam-looking address that said *Hello there, friend*. And then nothing else. I figured it was someone from college, trying to be funny. They kept sending the message until finally I replied a few days later. It bounced back. The email had been deleted. That happened some more off and on for about a month or two. Work was starting to really boom so it was just like this annoying little thing that happened, so I wasn't exactly focused on it." She sighed. The sound wobbled. She kept on.

"Then the hang-up calls on the landline in my house that I use for Greene Thumb and Hammer started. It went to my cell phone from there. I called one of the numbers back and it was disabled. Then, just like the emails, it stopped."

The box came next.

Bella was embarrassed to admit she'd never told anyone about it, even more so now, but the way Marco was homed in on her every word, the way his brow was drawn in concentration, seemed like a man who wasn't judging.

Just listening.

If sighing would have lessened the stress, she would have done it again.

But it wouldn't help.

It wouldn't fix what she should have done, just like it wouldn't stop what was happening now.

"A few months later, we had finished up a landscaping job for a client just outside Kelby Creek," Bella continued. "I was getting pictures of the finished project for our portfolio when I found a box with my name on it next to a portion of the fence we had installed. It was small and white, had one of those thin ribbons that people attach to helium balloons around it and a little stick-on tag with my name typed on it." She had a picture of it on her phone but Bella didn't stop. She needed to get it off her chest. All of it. "I thought it might be from the client but it was a napkin."

This time, Marco did speak up.

"A napkin? Was there anything on it?"

Bella nodded. She took one of the napkins from his tray, folded it in half, and put it between her lips. She pressed down and then released it.

She hadn't slept a wink since finding the message on the mirror. Something she'd tried to hide as she put makeup on before going to the department.

Now they were both looking at the dark peach lip print.

"It's something my mom always taught me to do after I put my lipstick on, after a meal, sometimes before getting a drink so I don't stain the glass more than needed," she explained.

"The napkin had a lip print," he spelled out.

"Not just any lip print. *Mine.* I *compared* mine to it when I got home."

"And they were the same?"

Bella nodded. "Like it was a mass-produced stamp."

"Was there anything else? In the box?"

She pointed to the note in his hand.

"A piece of paper with the same message. That was it."

Bella saw it then. A hint of emotion breaking through across the deputy's face. Tension. Anger.

And she hadn't even gotten to the worst part.

He opened his mouth to, she assumed, point out the obvious conclusion to jump to in her situation. Bella cut him off before he could. Even more, she reached out and touched his hand.

It was to still her nerves more than it was to make him realize she wasn't done.

He closed his mouth.

Back to impassive.

He wouldn't be for long.

"I thought maybe it was all someone messing with me. Or maybe that Kelby Creek is just becoming a place where people play awful pranks on each other. *But* then last night after we left Jennifer's house, well, I saw this." Bella went to the picture she'd taken on her phone. She gave it to the deputy with her free hand. He took it, not moving the other hand she was holding an inch.

"Where was this exactly?" Marco's voice was clipped. Tight.

"The bathroom mirror," she answered.

"But where?"

This time Bella let out another shaky breath. "In my bathroom. *In* my house."

Marco tensed. His nostrils flared. He clenched the jawline that would make most women's knees weak.

His eyes widened but only for a second.

It was his voice that changed the most though. No longer clipped. No longer impassive.

It was all emotion that he was no longer hiding.

He looked up from the phone and locked in on her.

Bella didn't know the man well but she swore she knew what he was going to say before he even uttered the words.

"Bella, you have a stalker."

Chapter Seven

There was no doctor, nurse or anyone else around to tell Marco he couldn't leave the hospital.

And he said as much to Carlos on the phone.

"I'm bringing her to the department and then we're going to her house," he told his partner as he pulled on the jeans he'd packed. When he went for his shirt, he cussed. "Scratch that, we're swinging by my place first so I can grab a shirt that's not destroyed. *Then* we're getting all of this sorted."

Carlos didn't try to tell him to stay put. He agreed to meet at the department and would call ahead to see if Detective Lovett was still there. Dawn County, Kelby Creek specifically, had a trove of cold cases. The number had only become higher after what had happened with Annie McHale during what locals, honest to God, all called The Flood. Marco thought that maybe what was happening to Bella could be connected to an older complaint of suspicious activity or stalking. Carlos had agreed.

Marco ended the call wearing his jeans, boots and the hospital gown. He'd been lucky that instead of forgetting a new shirt, he'd at least remembered to bring a jacket. His shoulder holster and service weapon went beneath it while he slipped his badge into his back pocket.

When he met Bella outside the door, she looked him up and down with a fleeting smile.

"I didn't know you were allowed to take the gowns with you."

Marco's sense of urgency had been climbing on top of itself the moment after Bella finished her recounting of someone stalking her. It was getting worse every second she was somewhere that he couldn't control, at least in some part. The hospital might have been considered small but right now it felt too big. Too open.

Too vulnerable.

It made Marco's skin crawl.

It also made him feel more protective.

Like he had on the hospital bed when his body reacted to hers on reflex.

Marco reached back and took her hand.

"They're just going to have to make an exception for this one," he said, already leading them to the elevator. "Worst-case, I'll pay them back."

Bella didn't say much but she also didn't complain about the contact. Her hand was warm and small, and how did it fit so perfectly in his? He didn't move at all as they waited in the elevator and, when she spoke, it had nothing to do with the fact that she was squeezing his hand back.

"What happens now? I mean, once we get to the department."

The elevator beeped off their passing of the second floor. Marco used his free hand to pull his jacket closed so it kept his gun out of sight. When they'd come in, the hospital had been all but dead. A few staff mulling around but, thankfully, no emergencies that had the building filled.

He hoped it was still just as dead.

Again, the feeling of being too vulnerable was eating at him.

"You'll do an official statement and timeline if you can and we'll go from there to see if we can find anything."

"And you'll go to my house? To make sure no one's there or there isn't some kind of hole in the wall where someone's secretly been living, right?" She was trying to use humor to undercut the fear. The same fear he now understood from the first day they'd met.

She'd thought it was him. The person leaving her the same message, over and over again.

Hello there, friend.

Marco had to admit that its creep factor rated high when used the way it had been.

"Yeah," he answered as the doors opened. "Carlos and I will make sure there's nothing going on there and see if we can't find some kind of clue."

She nodded and together they walked out into the parking lot with no one talking to or stopping them.

"My truck is over here," Bella said, pulling him gently in the opposite direction. They finally broke their contact but only after Marco held open the vehicle's door for her. He shut it and scanned the parking lot as he went to the passenger's side.

The lot was empty. The sky above them was not. It had darkened considerably since earlier that morning. Rain was coming. Marco could smell it in the air.

It only added to the ominous feeling starting to tangle with the urgency telling him that he wasn't waiting for the second shoe to drop—he was still waiting for the first real one to hit the floor. The boot to come crashing down.

And he didn't want Bella anywhere near it when that happened.

They drove in silence out of the parking lot. It didn't hold long.

"Aren't you going to ask me why I didn't tell anyone?"

Bella's voice was small. She kept her eyes focused on the road ahead.

Marco made sure to choose his words carefully.

"I think there are times when something happens that you don't expect, something that isn't *right*, and that *not* talking about it can help keep it from feeling real. I get it. I really do." He paused, then decided to go ahead and ask the first thought he'd had when she'd opened up to him. "What I don't really understand is, out of everyone—your family, friends and a department full of people—when you did speak up, you did it to me. Why?"

In profile Marco could see Bella tense. Just as he could see that tension leave in a sag of defeat. If she had planned to keep the answer to herself, it was a plan that didn't last long.

"Honestly? I think it's easier to open up to people who don't know you. Better to tell your innermost fears and anxieties to someone who has no comparison to your former self, I guess. *But*—" Bella sighed "—truth be told, I... Well, I trust you. I don't know why, I don't know *you*, but I can't seem to get around the feeling."

Marco was stunned into silence.

For many, many reasons.

It was only after he saw her in his periphery turn to him that he shook out a response.

"I guess you jumped the gun again, huh?"

Bella actually laughed.

"I guess I—"

The truck started to choke, shuddering and cutting Bella off.

"Not again!"

She put on her flashers and pulled off to the shoulder.

Marco was already on high alert when she flipped off the ignition. He had his hand hovering over the butt of his gun when she tried to restart it but nothing caught.

"Bella, is this what happened last time? The day we met?"

Marco was scanning their surroundings. They were on a street that had a storage-unit complex boasting air-conditioned units in the back, buildings on one side and a stretch of trees on the other. There were no cars on the road and only one car in the parking lot next to them at the storage-unit facility.

Again, like the hospital, it made him feel exposed. Vulnerable.

Unable to fully protect Bella if something went wrong.

Judging by her answer, Marco knew that something wrong was closer than further away.

"Yeah. I guess I never actually told you but the problem was—"

"Water or sugar mixed in the gas tank?" he interrupted.

Bella's eyes widened.

"How did you know?"

Marco unbuckled his seat belt, and he reached for his gun.

"I think I know what's happening," he hurried. "But I need to use your phone and let Carlos know—"

Marco didn't get a chance to pull out his gun.

Whatever slammed into the back of the truck crumpled any and all plans he was forming.

All Marco heard was Bella scream, then everything went dark.

"Marco? Oh, my God, Marco!"

Bella's seat belt was digging into her side. She couldn't figure out why at first.

Why was it digging into her right side so much? Why did she feel so weird?

And why wasn't Marco answering?

The details came in all at once.

They weren't kind.

The windshield was shattered but intact. She could see through it still, yet it wasn't the scene she'd last been looking at. There was no street ahead, only trees.

Trees facing the wrong way.

Then Bella put together why the seat belt was unforgiving against her chest and side. Also why she felt so weird.

The truck wasn't on four wheels anymore. It was on its side, the passenger's door against the ground and her door facing the darkening sky. The wrongness and pain was from gravity trying to pull Bella toward the ground.

Toward Marco.

"Marco?" she tried again. "Are you okay?"

Bella finally looked to her side and down.

She sucked in a breath just as her heart plummeted.

Marco had taken his seat belt off and because of that he was lying against the door pinned to the ground.

He wasn't moving.

"Marco?" Her voice was broken. Just like her truck around them. "Hang on. I'm coming."

He didn't stir.

Was he breathing?

She couldn't tell and she wouldn't find out if she stayed where she was.

Bella reached for the buckle at her hip and winced as pain scattered through her. She couldn't focus on it. She wouldn't. Not until she got to Marco. Adrenaline, and she was sure shock, helped her along. The second time she pushed the button, it released.

Gravity got its way and she dropped in an instant. It was a bad idea, which she should have realized before unbuckling. If Marco had been wearing his seat belt she would have smacked against him. Instead she managed to grab the seat to keep her full weight from hitting him.

Bella was even less graceful trying to move around him to stand. She ignored the blood that was on her arm, not knowing if it was his, hers or both.

Then she heard it.

A car door shutting.

Bella froze.

In her haste to help Marco, she'd glazed over one terrifying detail.

Someone had hit them. Hard. While they were parked on the shoulder of the street with their flashers on.

That couldn't be an accident, could it?

The message on the bathroom mirror blared to life in Bella's mind. Just as Marco's words in the hospital gave them sound.

Bella, you have a stalker.

Was it him?

Was he after her?

Bella reached on reflex for her cell phone in her pocket. It wasn't there. She'd put it in her cup holder when they'd gotten into the truck. The sound of footsteps echoed outside from near the back of the vehicle.

If adrenaline hadn't already been pulsing through her system, it would have been a new flood now.

Bella kept looking for her phone.

She could have cried in relief when she saw the time readout glowing near her feet. That meant it was still working. It was next to Marco's chest, next to the broken glass and dirt.

Bella was quick.

She didn't stop to check to see if Marco's chest was rising or falling, she didn't pause to think about calling her family first. All she was able to do was dial 9-1-1 and slip the phone into Marco's jacket pocket before she heard the footsteps turn into the noise of someone climbing.

Bella didn't know what else to do other than brace herself the best she could. She used her body to cover as much as Marco from view as she could and hoped against all hope that she was just being paranoid.

That it had been an accident and whoever had caused it was coming to help them.

That her stalker was terrifying but not the cause of this.

That it was just an awful coincidence.

But her hope shattered quite quickly.

A face came into view and she knew it wasn't about to get any better for them.

The man was wearing a mask. One she recognized from the movie *Scream*, only because her brother had bought the same one to wear almost every Halloween. White and twisted. Black eyes, black mouth.

Not something you wear to help someone crashed on the side of the road.

It wasn't fair.

It wasn't right.

And Bella had no options to fix any of it.

She liked to think she was a brave woman but she also believed that there were some situations that broke even the bravest.

Like being in a violent accident only to be greeted by a mask worn by a cult classic killer.

"Who—who are you?"

The masked man moved his head side to side, hanging down into the truck.

Bella wished the windshield had blown out from the impact or flip. She didn't know if she could drag Marco through it and into the trees if it had but she damn sure would have tried. There was no way to defend Marco or herself from her position.

"What do you want?"

The man disappeared for what only seemed

like a second. His hand, gloved, came into view
long enough to drop something.

Bella caught the paper on reflex.

Handwriting she was all too familiar with
spelled out one statement.

Come with me or he dies.

Chapter Eight

There must have been a patrol car nearby. Bella heard a siren before the mechanical gate to the storage-unit area closed behind them. The gate did nothing to block the sound, but the street, the wrecked car and Marco felt a world away.

Now it was just them. Bella and the masked man.

And he didn't seem bothered by the sound of the law coming closer.

In fact his body language was nothing but casual.

Minus the gun he was still holding.

Bella didn't know much about guns but knew shooting a moving target was often harder than one that willingly followed your every request.

Bella also knew what her father would tell her to do in her current situation. Mainly because he'd been coaching her for it most of her life.

If you're ever in a parking lot and someone tries to grab you, run around the car and yell, he'd told her during his first sit-down with her about safety tips. *If you can't do that, then yell your head off while you crawl under a car. You make yourself too much trouble for anyone to want to take you.*

Bella didn't have the chance to listen to either piece of advice, just as she couldn't use them now, but her father had spent years having this conversation off and on. So much so that she didn't actually need him there to have it again.

His voice came in as clear as the masked man's intent to have them go inside the air-conditioned storage building at the back of the property. The giant warehouse with enough places to stuff her if he had the urge to do so.

If you can't keep someone from catching you, then you don't let them take you, Bella, her dad had told her, the epitome of paternal severity. *Never ever let them put you in a vehicle. Once that happens, statistically, your chances of survival plummet.* He'd shaken his head. Then, during the first time he'd ever told her what to do just in case, he'd taken her hands in his and given her a smile that hurt. *And if they ever do take you, you make sure they don't keep you. Even if they have a weapon, even if they're bigger and meaner, you fight or you run as hard as you can. No matter how scary it might be, you make them regret ever thinking they had a shot of keeping Bella Greene.*

The walk up to the storage-unit building was a straight line from the main gate. On either side were two rows of the outdoor units, all orange-and-blue doors closed and locked. The main office was next to the main gate but on the opposite side of it. If anyone was inside, if anyone had seen what happened, no one made a peep.

Bella had hoped for a longer walk from the gate to the building but it felt like only seconds.

She stopped next to the main door inside. Her father's voice rang through her mind as she spoke to the masked man.

"It needs a code to open." She pointed to the keypad next to the door. It was one of the main reasons the storage facility was open at all times. No one could get in unless they were clients.

Bella glanced down at the gun. It was still in his hand but not aimed at her. She made sure to keep her eyes on it as he moved to the keypad. To add to the list of surprises that were making up her day, the masked man typed in a code.

And it worked.

The door beeped, unlocked, and the man opened it.

He turned back toward her and motioned her past him.

Bella could feel the wave of cool air come out of the building. She could smell the staleness of a building rarely frequented. The fluorescent lights came on because of the motion sensors and showed a clean, shiny painted concrete floor.

It was a nice building. Not a terrible place to be under normal circumstances.

But Bella loved her dad a whole, whole lot, which meant there was no way in the world she was going to go inside of it.

With what her brother had once called sneaky speed, Bella kicked out at the man.

He hadn't expected that.

Her foot connected with his groin and, mask or not, he was like every other man who'd been kicked there. He let out a groan and all reflexes went to him trying to process the pain while attempting to protect himself so it wouldn't happen again. He bent over, gun still in his hand but now pointed away, and staggered back past the door.

Bella didn't waste her small opening.

She turned on her heel so fast that she kicked up dirt. Then she was running toward the gate with everything she had, already planning to hang the first right she could around a row of units so she could hide.

But then something odd happened.

Something that slammed the brakes on her fight-or-flight response.

The masked man yelled out but not in pain. It was for her.

"Bella!"

His voice echoed around her.

His voice.

It stopped her in her tracks, like a slap to the face.

She turned around, chest heaving up and down as she tried to breathe.

She knew that voice.

She *knew* it, right?

The man was in the doorway still. Mask on, gun at his side. With his other hand, he went to the bottom of his mask.

Was he about to take it off?

"Bella!"

This time, Bella recognized the voice instantly.

And it was coming from behind her at the gate.

"Get down!" And then to the man: "Drop the gun! Now!"

Bella hit the dirt and covered her head. She closed her eyes tight as the sound of gunshots exploded around her.

It only took a second or two.

Then the world was quiet again.

Bella lifted her head only enough to look at the second man to call her name.

Her heart squeezed.

It was Marco and what a sight he was to see.

Standing a few feet from her, he had his legs braced apart, and his gun aimed ahead without any part of him wavering. His jaw was hard, his eyes were focused, and even though he looked like he had seen better days, thanks to cuts and blood across his body, Bella only felt strength from him now.

Even as he spoke, it was all steel and gunpowder.

"Bella, come to me now."

She didn't have to be told twice.

Bella was off the ground and running to him like she'd been practicing for this her whole life. The moment she was near him, he took her hand and spun them both around.

The gate wasn't all the way open but there was a new gap that hadn't been there before.

Marco pushed her through it, then pulled her to the other side of the concrete beam it attached to. There they were, facing the street, her truck in the distance, with the main office to their side.

"Are you hurt?" Marco asked, pushing her gently against the concrete.

Bella shook her head.

"Are you? Did you get shot?"

The strength she'd seen only seconds before had done a one-eighty. Now Bella could read the pain in his expression as clearly as she could see the blood.

"No. He's a poor shot but I think I could have gotten him. He ran inside that building. Which is why—" Marco stumbled to the side. Bella had to throw her arms out to steady him. He kept on like it hadn't happened. "Which is why you're going to take my gun."

"Why don't you keep your gun?" she asked, alarmed.

Marco didn't look happy with the answer he was about to give.

"Because I think I'm about to pass out."

True to his word, the second she took the gun from him, Marco started to go slack. It was all Bella could do to slide down to the ground with him, trying desperately to keep her hand and legs between him and the ground.

"Marco? Marco?"

The deputy didn't answer. All she could hear now was a siren getting louder.

It was only after the sheriff's deputy patrol car came to a screeching halt on the street between them and her truck did Bella realize a heart-squeezing detail.

With his back to her chest, Marco had positioned himself in between her and anyone coming their way.

Even unconscious he was still trying to protect her.

THE RAIN CAME. A thunderstorm rode into town and turned severe just after everyone showed up at the hospital. At least, that was the best Marco could figure how it played out.

After falling unconscious, he'd woken up in the back of an ambulance, a whole two minutes away from Haven. When Bella wasn't next to him, he'd pitched a fit. Then Carlos had met him when they'd gotten to their destination and assured Marco she was safe with the sheriff and would be there soon.

The rain started pouring then. It beat against the roof and walls while the thunder shook the windows and showed him a day that had turned dark. Even though that had already happened before the storm.

"We have everyone looking for him," Carlos said, trying to assure Marco before the doctor came in. He was talking about the masked man. The one who had sent Marco to the hospital. Twice. "We'll get him," Carlos added. "Until then, we're going to make sure you and Bella are safe."

His definition of safe was a deputy and a hospital security officer positioned in the hallway of the third floor. But only after Marco had a CAT scan done and that was only after he'd gotten stitches. Ten along his chest.

It was those stitches he was looking down at when he got his first visitor since being moved.

Though it wasn't whom he had hoped it would be.

And it definitely wasn't even someone on his top-five list of possibilities.

"Can I come in?"

Grantham Greene, called Grant as Marco knew, was already walking in before he could be invited. Marco didn't mind.

He said as much and motioned to one of the chairs next to the bed. Unlike his daughter, Grant decided to sit in one of them instead of next to Marco on the bed.

"Bella wanted me to let you know that she'll be in here as soon as she's done," he started. "The sheriff was talking to her and a detective is with her now. Detective Love or whatever his name is. The new guy before you showed up."

"Detective Lovett. He's good. I like him." Marco couldn't deny he was disappointed that Bella wasn't there but he was also relieved. Before Foster had come to Kelby Creek, he'd been a hotshot detective in Seattle. When he'd come back to his hometown, his fame had only grown after he'd put to bed a town-wide investigation. Having him on the case would only strengthen their chances of finding the masked man.

And Marco was going to find him, all right.

"Is she okay?" Marco asked, hoping he didn't betray every inch of concern he had. "Deputy Park said she was but, well, I haven't seen her yet."

Grant gave a nod that became a shrug.

"She's worried about you and still a bit scared but, physically she's okay. A nasty cut on her arm but she managed to not need stitches." His gaze went to Marco's bare chest and the bandage over the stitches he definitely had needed. "That's probably going to scar. How about the rest of you? Bella said you had to get a CT?"

Marco felt oddly at ease with Grant Greene so he answered honestly instead of deciding not to share.

"I have a concussion from the wreck—that's why they think I passed out. Twice." He sighed. "It's also why I'm in observation here until I'm told otherwise."

Grant nodded again.

It was a slow, thoughtful movement that turned into silence.

He'd come to say something. Marco waited.

After a moment, Grant was ready.

"Do you know the story of what happened

to Annie McHale? What everyone around here refers to as The Flood?"

Marco nodded.

"I know what most of the country knows after the story went viral. And the details the sheriff filled me in on when I got the job here. But, to be fair, I haven't heard it from a true local. Someone who was outside of law enforcement or the media."

Grant seemed to approve of that answer.

"Then let me be the first local who lived through it to tell you." He leaned forward so his elbows were on his knees and his hands were domed between them. "And when I'm done, then you're going to tell me exactly why *you* came to Kelby Creek. Or else you, Mr. Rossi, will never see my daughter again."

Chapter Nine

"My wife and I were born in Kelby Creek and decided to stay in it when we found out we were pregnant with Bella."

Grant hadn't skipped a beat since issuing his threat. Marco hadn't stopped him to talk about that same threat either. Instead both were focused on the story. Marco more so than Bella's father. The Flood had become a national story and, in its wake, had nearly destroyed an entire town.

Hearing the details that hadn't been in the newspapers or weren't part of some conspiracy theory posted online was a welcome change for Marco.

"We were also extremely broke," Grant continued. "I was taking care of my mother at the time and my wife had no living family left so there was no one to help us, or to reach out to, but us. I worked two jobs and she worked long shifts and, still, some days it felt like we weren't living, just surviving. That kind of stress was grinding. Even though I didn't want it, that kind of stress turned into resentment, for me, really quick. Especially for people who had a lot of money they did almost nothing to get. Then, one day, I met Arthur McHale and my resentment at the rich in this town went away." Grant sighed. Then smiled for the briefest of seconds.

"See, Arthur was a nice guy. So was his wife. They could have lived out their days not doing a thing and still with enough money to support them and theirs for another generation or two, but instead they invested back into Kelby Creek. They put money in the town and community and were active in seeing that they helped it grow. The McHales could have been one of those rich families you see on TV or movies who don't care about the poor around them, but that wasn't their style at all. They were kind and smart and never missed an opportunity to help and everyone loved them for it. Even their kid was like them in all of the best ways."

There was no hint of a smile now. Not even for the briefest of seconds.

"That's why when Annie went missing, it became a town full of people trying their best to find her. And, when the ransom call came in, even though it wasn't our kid, we all wanted a piece of whoever had had the audacity to take her. We took it personally." He moved his hands from being domed to resting on top of his knees. A tell for someone who was trying to seem like he wasn't angry. That he was in control. His hands fisted once and then relaxed. He continued with a bit more heaviness to his words. "You know what happens next."

"The ransom call asking for money to be exchanged at a park," Marco supplied. "The sheriff and some undercover deputies went with Mr. McHale to deliver it. The sheriff was Annie's godfather, right?" Grant nodded. "Then it was a bloodbath," Marco added. "Five people died and several were injured."

"Bloodbath is a phrasing that's more accurate than some I've read," he said. "A Georgia paper called it a small trap, but there was nothing small about it. Bella said you met Justin? Our current client."

"Briefly."

Grant's frown deepened, becoming more severe.

"Him and his wife were there. In the park. No one was supposed to be but, according to the sheriff, there wasn't enough time to clear everyone and, even if they did, it would raise suspicions. So when the kidnappers opened fire on the deputies, they also opened fire on Justin and Carla."

Marco didn't need him to spell the outcome out based on his body language but Grant did all the same.

"She died in his arms at that park and Annie McHale was still nowhere to be found."

"The video was next, right?" Marco recalled the grainy footage he'd seen on the internet once the story had gone viral. "Of Annie somewhere, tied up."

"Yeah. Uploaded to our town's official website. The mayor, also the best of friends with the McHales, tried to get it removed but it took a while. By then Annie had grabbed the FBI's attention. They sent a set of partners here to get to the bottom of it."

Grant sighed again. In just retelling the story, he seemed to have grown more tired. Marco wanted to help him get to where he was going without doing it all on his own.

"I was told that one of the FBI agents, Ortega I think was her name, told her partner she found a lead but then disappeared. He looked for her but a storm came and he found the mayor instead," Marco said, trying to remember the details.

Grant swore under his breath.

"We call it The Flood because a flash flood warning had been issued and the mayor was such a bad driver when the sun was shining that he didn't stand a chance on the roads during it," he said. "He ran off the road and the FBI agent just happened to come up on him. He was trying to help him when the agent saw something that had flown loose during the wreck. A necklace. Annie's necklace."

"That's when he figured it out," Marco guessed. "That's when the agent realized the mayor was connected."

"Yep. He opened his own investigation in secret and, well, you know the rest."

"The sheriff and mayor were the ones who came up with the abduction and ransom—"

"—and when a new FBI task force showed up to figure out how far their corruption led, they were able to nearly shut down every law enforcement and government position in town. The guilty were either caught, killed while trying to flee or managed to leave town and hide. Annie was never found. Neither was Ms. Ortega."

Grant shook his head.

"The people with the most power in this town, with the most respect, used all of us for one selfish reason or another," he said, anger etched into every word. "They used our trust to their advantage and, at the end of the day, we paid the price."

His eyes moved to the table next to the bed

and found Marco's badge. It was resting on top of his holster.

"They did good things, the people who broke our trust," he continued, looking back at him. "But good deeds don't cancel out bad apples. And just because you saved my daughter, something I will always be grateful for, doesn't mean you're not one of those bad apples." Grant was finally at the reason why he'd given Marco a history lesson. He squared up his shoulders and his gaze never wavered once he continued.

"So I need you to tell me why you came to Kelby Creek and why any of us should trust you."

THE MASKED MAN hadn't been caught. Once he'd gone into the storage building, he'd all but disappeared. It had seemed to weigh on Detective Lovett when he went through every detail of their terrifying adventure and then backtracked to Bella's escalating messages.

It was there in the hospital, talking with a relative stranger—something that was becoming all too common—that Bella found out the truth behind Marco's earlier accident. The reason why they'd been in the hospital only that morning.

She'd been under the impression the hit-and-run had been an accident, but Detective Lovett wondered if it wasn't her close proximity with

Marco that had put him on the masked man's radar for the first attack.

Bella had been unable to hide her surprise, though the detective had taken it as offense instead.

"I didn't mean this happened because of you," he'd tacked on. "I'm just saying that from my experience with stalkers, sometimes obsession can turn into trying to get rid of threats. Romantic threats."

He'd swept his gaze down to his notes on the last part. Bella was thankful for the quick privacy. Mainly because she didn't know which emotion had sprung up across her face.

From there they didn't talk too much more. He got all of her information and Bella was becoming more and more restless. Detective Lovett did, however, leave her with something that eased a mind already becoming afraid again.

"Until we find him, and we will find him, we're going to station a car outside your house for surveillance. But, if you want to stay with your family, we'll also station a car at whatever house you end up going to."

Bella sighed. More from being tired at how stressed she knew she was going to be that night.

"You saw my family come into the hospital

when you first got here, right?" she asked. "The big loud blob that turned into a massive hug? There's no way my father lets me stay anywhere other than my parents' house. That or everyone is going to come to mine."

Detective Lovett chuckled.

"To be honest, if I were a father, I'd do the same. Just call me with where you decide to stay and we can have someone go there."

Bella agreed and, seconds after the detective was out of the room, she was up and hurrying to the third floor. She hadn't seen Marco since he'd come in and it was bothering her. *Really* bothering her.

Recounting everything that had happened had only watered a seed of worry and urgency within her. Seeing Marco in the truck, not knowing if he was dead, and then having him save her only to pass out in her arms?

It was too much.

Too much without seeing him.

Without making sure he was okay.

So Bella didn't stop to check herself in the mirror or make nice, polite chitchat with the deputy in the hall, the nurse in the elevator she'd gone to high school with or even her father, who was leaving Marco's room right as she got there. Though she did pause long enough to listen to what her father reached out to her to say.

"He's doing good," he said with a smile. "A little bandage on his chest but good. I think all he'll need is a little rest after this. A good home-cooked meal too. But he's going to be fine. He's tough."

But tough wasn't the same as indestructible.

And Bella needed to see him.

To hear it from Marco himself that he was okay.

Yet it wasn't until she was in the room with the deputy that something shifted. That the way she felt about the man changed.

It only helped matters that the moment he saw her, he was smirking.

"I think your dad just—" But Marco didn't get a chance to finish.

Bella had been cleared by the doctor and deemed lucky to only have a few cuts across her from the accident. She had some bandages but that was it. No leg injuries. No impaired movement. Not even a reason to take pain meds.

Which made it all the easier to get to the bed in record time. It was even easier to reach out to him, take his face in her hands and pull him into a kiss.

One she hadn't meant to do.

One she hadn't even *thought* to do when she'd come in.

Yet one she absolutely needed.

Bella reveled in the warmth of his lips and how forgiving they were despite the surprise. They melted against hers without resistance. But this kiss wasn't about pleasure.

It was about relief.

Relief and being grateful.

Bella ended it as quickly as she started it and stepped back, somehow breathless despite how brief the whole interaction had been.

Marco's lips were still parted. His eyebrow rose.

"I'm glad you're okay," Bella said, simply.

Marco leaned back again. He was smiling.

"Not only am I okay, I'm very awake now."

Bella felt the relief and gratefulness burn away in a blush that heated the whole of her. She stood by the kiss but now the awkwardness was making its way in too.

"I—I'm sorry," she said in a rush. "It's just, uh, in my defense you saved my life and, well, it's very hard not to kiss someone who's saved your life."

Marco actually laughed. It made the blush running amok through her body heat up even more.

He waved his hand through the air.

"Listen, I'm just glad your dad took a different approach."

Bella tilted her head to the side in question.

"What exactly did he say when he was in here?"

Marco's smile transformed into a grin.

"Well, apparently, since I passed his trust test, that means he's allowed to threaten me."

Bella felt her eyes narrow.

What had her father done?

"Threaten you with what?"

Marco chuckled. He sat up, adopted what she could only assume was his impression of her father and pointed at her with a sternness that *definitely* was her dad.

"Southern hospitality."

Chapter Ten

Carlos dropped him off at the curb like Marco was going to a sleepover and Deputy Park was his father. The deputy must have thought the same thing, as he rolled the passenger-side window down and called through it.

"Don't stay up too late or you'll be cranky tomorrow." Carlos said it with a smile. It made Marco chuckle.

He was careful as he moved his duffel bag from one hand to the other. His stitches wouldn't pull from such a small task but he wanted to make absolutely sure he didn't have a reason to go back to the hospital.

Not again.

At least, not for the third time in twenty-four hours.

He didn't think his sanity or his insurance could handle it.

"Sure thing, Dad," Marco returned. "Just

make sure you leave your phone on in case we need to talk."

Carlos laughed. Then he sobered. It was no longer a joking matter. He nodded toward the patrol car parked out front against the curb. Dawn County Sheriff's Deputy was printed along the side. There was one man behind the wheel, his badge no doubt pinned to his uniform.

"That's Cooper," Carlos said. "He's night shift and one heck of a determined guy. Good at the details too. I put his number in that new phone of yours if you need him for whatever reason. He'll change out with me in the morning and I can update you then on what's happening. That good?"

Marco didn't think any of this was good but he appreciated the concern and consideration Carlos kept giving him.

If he were being honest, it was something he sorely had missed since the incident at his last department.

"That works. Just shoot me a text when you're out here and I'll come meet you."

"Ten-four."

They said their goodbyes and Marco made eye contact with Cooper through his windshield. They exchanged nods and then Marco was walking up to a front porch covered in ceramic gnomes of varying colors, shapes and themes. It was a far cry from his nondescript apartment, that was for sure.

The front door flew open before Marco could knock.

Bella Greene smiled back at him, a bit rosy-cheeked and breathless.

"I still can't believe you agreed to do this." She waved her arms around to include the general house behind them. "I *had* to be here but you definitely didn't. If you thought me being awkward and intrusive during our dinner at the restaurant the other day was bad, then you're in for a treat. A really unsettling, loud treat."

Marco laughed.

"It's not like your dad gave me much of a choice," he said. "He didn't right out threaten me with what he'd do if I turned down the offer but I'm good at reading between the lines. And between his lines told me to accept staying here for the night with grace instead of trying to get out of it."

Whether it was his imagination or the poor lighting from the rustic lantern fixed to the wall or the darkness of night around them, Marco almost thought he saw a look of disappointment cross Bella's face. He didn't get a chance to clear the air to let her know that he was grateful. That had Grant not asked him in, he would have been alone. And while he'd grown accustomed to that, after the day he'd had, Marco found he didn't want to be alone just yet.

The man himself popped up behind Bella, beer in one hand and the only other Greene family member that Marco hadn't yet met holding the other.

Valerie Greene was an older version of her daughter in beauty *and* volume. She beamed as she greeted him.

"You made it just in time, Deputy Rossi! I hope you like lasagna!"

THE GREENE FAMILY home was an interesting collection of rooms, colors and architecture. Marco could tell the house was older and yet some parts of it seemed absolutely brand-new. It was something that Bella must have realized he'd picked up on because she smiled and motioned to the stairs that were tucked just inside the entryway.

"My dad's been renovating this house since my parents got it from his mother after she passed." Bella ran her hand along the stair railing. "It's why Val and I didn't realize in school that not everyone spent their weekends and some nights renovating different rooms of their house. For us it was always normal to be installing new flooring, replumbing and learning the hard way that we're really bad at grouting things." She nodded up the stairs. Her hair was loose and managed to shimmer beneath the LED lights in the entryway. "My parents like their privacy and have a suite behind the kitchen. All other rooms are up here. Follow me."

Bella led him upstairs to the second-floor landing, which was as nice as the downstairs. The walls were soothing in color, the floors were hardwood and shone, and weird little knickknacks that oddly worked in the space dotted shelves and nooks along the way. But what Marco liked more than the nice furnishings and surroundings were all the pictures.

Photographs of the Greene family stretched across every available inch of wall. Like wallpaper that could easily be rearranged when the desire struck them. Marco recognized younger versions of everyone he'd met; most notable, though, was Bella. Marco had to stop and press his finger against a small frame next to the first closed door in the hallway.

"Is this you wearing a tutu and holding on to a jackhammer?"

Bella laughed. Her cheeks tinted again.

"If it's not, then I have several questions for my family." That laugh had turned into a smile that was sitting pretty across those lips. He was starting to see that Bella had a knack for dealing with stress. Or at least compartmentalizing it. That didn't mean the fear, the worry and the stress weren't still there though. While he was enjoying seeing a smiling, happy Bella, a part of him wanted to see the other side. The one she hid, whether it was for pride or self-preservation or simply because she thought she had to. He wanted to see it and to help her through it.

He wanted her to be happy, more and more with each passing exchange between them.

Once again Marco found himself wondering who Bella had been before he'd come to town. Before she started getting the messages from the masked man. Before she'd come back to Kelby Creek. He even wondered what she'd been like as a teen.

He wondered so much about Bella that he realized that in itself was significant. Yet, standing in the upstairs hallway of her parents' house after such an intense day, Marco knew now wasn't the time to deep dive into who Bella Greene had been and was currently.

So he stayed with his jokes. He tried to be charming and smile and laugh and pretend like he was on a normal tour of her family's house and that he was staying in their guest bedroom only because he had nowhere else to go. Even though he did. It just happened to be a long lonely way across town. Again, something that normally wouldn't bother him but was now pricking at his skin.

Bella added on to her sarcastic answer with the real one, never the wiser to his ongoing internal battle between staying a loner and wanting to get closer to her.

"Despite not really getting into construction as a job until after I came back to Kelby Creek, I actually had always really wanted to use a jackhammer." She shrugged. "Some girls dream of doing dance or following boy bands and going to concerts where they have really nice hair and somewhat provocative PG-13 dance moves, but me? I had seen the movie *Tremors* with Kevin Bacon, and at the very beginning, you have two construction workers who are using a jackhammer to break up the road. For some reason, I couldn't get over how cool it was to watch that little thing break up something as hard and sturdy as a road, and I became obsessed. Every birthday after that I told my dad all I wanted was to use a jackhammer."

"Well, it looks like dreams come true. Though I have to ask, did the tutu come with it or was that your own personal touch?"

Bella laughed again.

"I was on the way to a birthday party that had a theme," she said. "I don't remember exactly what the theme was or who even threw it because right before the party Dad brought me to the garage and there was this beaut. He had to rent it for the week to do work on the kitchen floor." Bella grinned. "I'd like to say that I took that picture and then went to my party like any normal kid would but…"

"Please tell me you skipped the kid's birthday party just to use a jackhammer."

Bella shrugged and walked through the door.

"I'll let you use your imagination on that one."

They were standing in the guest bedroom that Grant had all but pushed on Marco at the hospital. It was quaint, clean and more room than he had expected to be given. The bed was a queen, there was a love seat at its foot and a door that he believed led to a bathroom.

"This is nicer than my apartment," he said. "Can I get Greene Thumb and Hammer to come to my apartment and do some renovations? I'm sure my landlord won't mind the upgrade."

Bella took his bag from his hand and placed it on the dresser against the wall. Marco noted she was just as careful to take it as he had been to move it from one hand to the other.

"You're all for praising us now but just wait until we actually sit down to eat." Bella did an overdramatic sigh. "Remember when I accused you of having armor around your heart? I only had the audacity to say such a corny thing because I grew up with this bunch. You just entered the house of cheesy '80s lines and fortune-cookie jargon. And football talk. Alabama football, to be exact."

The smile and humor Bella had been projecting wavered as her eyes glanced out the window. Marco followed her gaze, adrenaline dangerously close to rising, but all he saw was a backyard. Fenced in, barely lit and void of anyone or anything. When he turned back around, he could tell she realized she'd been caught. That an emotion had broken through her courtesy and curiosity. If only for a second.

This time Marco decided not to let the moment go without probing. Not after everything they'd been through just within the last twenty-four hours.

"This seems like a really obvious question, but I have to ask, what's wrong?" Marco moved so his body was between her and the window. He kept his eyes firmly on hers, hoping that she saw he was as invested in the answer as he was in asking the question.

Bella didn't immediately respond. At least, not with her words. She did, however, point down to the floor.

When she spoke, it was soft, quiet.

"Everyone I love is in this house," she said,

simply. "If someone really wants me, if that masked man is obsessed with me, isn't my being with all of you putting you in danger? More danger than we were in earlier? Am I just putting the largest of targets on my family's back?"

Marco had actually waited for this exact conversation. When he told her in the hospital that he'd accepted her father's invitation to stay that night, Marco had seen that Bella wasn't a fan of the idea. But not because of him. She hadn't like it because of her staying there too. Marco understood her reservations and knew he couldn't completely remove them but that didn't mean he didn't want to squash them. If only a little.

"*You* are not doing anything."

Marco took her hands in his, hoping the contact fastened her to him.

"None of this, none of what has happened, is or ever will be your fault," he continued. "Someone else's obsession has become dangerous and that's my job. That's the department's job. We do our best to stop the danger and keep those who are in it safe. While no one should or can tell you how to feel, I think it's best if you try really hard to let go of that guilt, that worry, and give it to me for now." He smiled, dropped one of her hands and pointed down at the floor like she had. "Because all I know is that beneath our feet is a family who would do anything to protect you and each other—" Marco pointed to the wall that faced the front of the house "—a sheriff's department that is personally and completely invested in keeping you, us and your family safe—" then Marco pointed to himself "—and a deputy who is also personally and completely invested in not only keeping everyone safe but has proved that he cannot be easily sidelined when it comes to protecting you."

He shrugged, trying to show he was nonchalant when in fact his heartbeat had started to speed up. Marco wanted, needed, to prove that Bella was safe with him even though they'd been attacked.

"I don't think that masked man will be coming here tonight," he added. "In fact I can't imagine he's even still in town after what happened. But, on the off chance that he has the gall to try something, I don't think he'll even make it past the front door. I'll make sure of that."

Bella's eyes flitted down to his lips but she nodded.

"Okay."

It was such a small and simple and quiet answer that his heartbeat went from picking up speed to a gallop. Because there was one detail they had both skipped over during their limited conversation at the hospital. One that he now fully felt standing in Bella's childhood home, staring into her icy blues and holding her hand.

"Did you hear why the department and ambulance got to us so quickly after the wreck? Why the first patrol car got there within five minutes?"

Bella shook her head.

"No. I just assumed they were close."

"They weren't actually. Instead they were flooring it to us because the dispatcher heard you." Marco felt the smile but had no idea if he was hiding the emotion behind it. "She heard you say that a deputy was down and needed immediate medical attention or he could die. She *also* heard you tell the man that you would come along with him so he wouldn't shoot me." He let out a small breath. Marco didn't know if Bella knew enough about him by now to hear how he was equally in awe and proud.

So he made sure he showed her after he explained.

"You must've only had a minute, maybe less, to react after he hit us and you used every second of that and made them count. You could've also found a way to protect yourself but, instead, you protected me."

Marco put his hand up to Bella's cheek. Her skin was warm against the palm of his hand. Their second kiss was just as soft, sweet and brief as their first. Yet this time it was Marco who started and then ended it.

And he was more than aware of how little he wanted to end it.

Bella's eyelashes fluttered up, dark against her rosy cheeks. Her lips were still parted when he recalled back to the first time they had touched like this.

"You're right," he said. "It *is* hard not to kiss someone who's saved your life."

Chapter Eleven

Dinner wasn't that bad. At least it wasn't what Bella had expected it to be. Which, she realized, was starting to be the constant in her current life. Things she didn't expect and everything else that happened after.

When she was a teenager, Bella had had a boy over to meet her family. His name was Rodney and he was as shy as the day was long. He'd done everything a boy trying to impress her parents was supposed to do. He'd shaken her father's hand, complimented her mother's cooking and made harmless jokes at her expense to try to win over Val. Yet, nothing had really clicked. Her father had been suspicious and openly wondered what his intentions were, her mother hadn't liked Rodney making jokes at her expense just to score points with Val, and her brother had never really told her why he wasn't a fan of Rodney other than he wasn't.

"You just get a feeling sometimes, Bella,"

he'd said. "And the feeling I got with him was that he's a high school mistake you should avoid making."

Since then Bella had always been a bit concerned with bringing people over to the house. Her parents thought it was because she was embarrassed by them, of how they had a hard time keeping their thoughts to themselves, but the truth was Bella often found herself persuaded to her family's point of view, negative or not. She knew if her family didn't like someone that, even though she was her own woman with her own opinions and thoughts and experiences, having the people she cared about the most decide to not be in someone's corner meant that she too would eventually decide the same thing. So instead of chancing that, she decided not to bring over anyone else since Rodney—at least, no potential boyfriends or romantic interests.

But now there was Marco.

They were in a completely different situation than when she was a teenager and bringing a boy over, yet here Bella was, stomach tight with nerves, as they settled around the dining room table she'd grown up eating at. Next to a man she was starting to get to know through a terrifying crash course that was a football field's length away from normal.

A man who had kissed her and then managed

to walk away like his heart wasn't about to beat through his chest.

Bella had been afraid that any goodwill or feelings her family had had for the deputy would change over the course of one very delicious lasagna.

Thankfully, nothing of the sort happened.

"Wait, wait, wait a minute," Val said, hand holding a fork out, and pointed at Marco across the table from him. "You got there and this guy had no pants on but was wearing whipped cream instead?"

Marco laughed, something he was doing a lot more of since devouring two chunks of Valerie Greene's infamous homemade lasagna.

"No joke," he said. "Apparently he was trying to be funny and romantic for his ex-girlfriend, who, also apparently, wasn't a fan of the gesture. I had to bring him into the department and then spent the next few hours cleaning my patrol car. You'll never believe such a small guy could make such a big mess."

Val howled with laughter. Bella took a sip of her wine. While Marco talked, she occasionally studied her parents' expressions to see if they were unimpressed with the deputy. Everyone was all smiles though, even Justin, who had made the trip to the house at the request of her father.

As he'd gotten Bella's call from the hospital, her father had managed to lose his keys in his haste to leave the site of Justin's shed. It was only luck that Justin had been working from home that day and had been kind enough to drive him and Val. He'd also been kind enough to offer a handful of security cameras that ran off an application now on her father's phone. Something to give them a temporary peace of mind while they all ordered their own security systems for each of their houses.

Marco, Val and Justin had set up the cameras on loan right after Bella and the deputy's quick kiss. It had been weirdly cute to see the three of them palling around. When Justin went home for the night, they even hung out on the front porch, talking about who knew what before parting ways.

It made Bella wonder if Marco wasn't as much of a loner as she'd once thought.

"All right, I don't know about y'all but I'm exhausted and I didn't even do anything today except worry," her mother announced once the table was cleared and the dishes were done. Valerie Greene was all about creating order in the chaos as a way to keep herself sane. They could be in the middle of a tornado warning and she'd be folding laundry to keep her nerves in check. It was also why they'd had her lasagna instead of something easier like a pizza or ordering in. Bella's mom deep dived into domestic distraction when things got bumpy. She was almost sure that the kitchen would be spotless by the morning. "So, I know you two need some sleep."

She made a whooshing motion with a hand towel toward the stairs but not before pulling Bella into a hug that she felt all the way into her bones.

"I'm so glad you're okay, my sweet Bells," she said to Bella's hair. "I don't know what I would do if something happened to you. To any of you."

Bella patted her mother's back.

"I know. I'm okay though, Mom. I promise."

They ended the embrace and then Marco was in her sights. She was more careful at putting her arms around him. While he'd been cleared by the doctor to leave the hospital, there was no getting around the fact that he had seen better days. There was also no denying that he was tired. Even his speech was starting to thicken. Bella had no idea when the last time was that he'd slept.

"And you," her mother said as she stepped back again. "If there's anything you need, anything you *ever* need, you don't hesitate to come get us. You understand?"

Marco nodded.

"Yes, ma'am, I understand."

Bella's father expressed his feelings with a handshake to Marco and a quick hug to her. Then he turned to Val and pointed toward the stairs too.

"You're gonna stay the whole night and not sneak out to go back to your house," he scolded. "I don't care if you think you're some big bad adult, tonight all of my children are under my roof. You got it?"

Bella stifled a laugh. Their father was using his I'm-raising-two-teenagers voice. She had to admit it was still effective, even as an adult.

Val rolled his eyes. He agreed.

"I already said I was going to stay," he added. "I'm not going to skip the chance to get home-made pancakes from Mom tomorrow. And, for future reference, you can just lead with that instead of trying to act tough."

He laughed all the way up the stairs as their father tried to chase him. Her mother caught their father by the belt loop and pulled him in the direction of their bedroom, chuckling as she went.

Marco walked Bella to the room across from his. The same one that she'd grown up in. He stopped just inside the door and looked around, his eyebrow raised.

"This room used to be a lot more chaotic," she offered before he could ask why it was obviously not a bedroom anymore. "Or at least chaotic in the way of how many stuffed animals and posters of the Backstreet Boys it used to have. It's Dad's office now but the daybed sleeps like a dream. Which was nice when I stayed here for a while after I was laid off and came back to town. If I'm not mistaken, there are plans to make Val's old room into a gym next. Even though we have our own homes in town, this piece of news still offends him. He tried to have a vote last family supper to change their minds. I haven't had the heart to tell him yet that Mom already said it's been decided and the treadmill comes in at the end of the month."

Marco grinned at that.

"My parents would fight me and my sister tooth and nail if we ever told them they needed to pack up our childhood things. They moved once Amy and I left the nest and they still set up bedrooms for us in the new house, just in case we ever wanted them."

Bella softened and let out an *aww*.

"That's kind of really sweet."

He shrugged.

"Occasionally they overcompensate to make sure that we know they love us. Amy calls it a great hazard of being adopted from foster care.

They're always trying to be our family, even though they're already there."

It was only the second time that Marco had spoken about his family. This time, however, Bella wanted more. She wanted to ask questions that would define him, that would make her understand him better, and that would show him that he was becoming more than just someone who was interesting to her. More than some shiny new object in town. But the timing, like so many other instances in their short acquaintanceship, was off.

She let the comment stay just as a series of rhythmic beeps and buzzes came from his pocket. Marco pulled out his phone.

"Speaking of my family, this is Amy," he said. "And knowing her, this will take a while."

"Oh, that's no problem," Bella hurried. "I'm just about to turn in anyway. I'll see you in the morning."

Marco answered the phone and was in the guest bedroom before Bella could think of something else to better end the night with. There was a restlessness in her. She wanted to say more, to do more, but there were only so many hours in the day. Plus, they all really did need to rest, Marco more than any of them.

Still, Bella was slower than usual getting ready for bed. Like she were a teenager again, she fought the immature urge to listen really hard as she walked by his bedroom door to the hall bathroom, trying to see if he was still awake.

Leave the man alone, she mentally chided herself after the third pass by. *Just because you kissed him and he kissed you, doesn't mean you need to keep thinking about kissing now.*

It was a ridiculous little pep talk but it did the trick. Bella finally laid down as ten o'clock rolled around.

But then eleven o'clock came.

And then midnight.

Bella could no more sleep than she could stop thinking about everything that had happened. About Marco. About the masked man.

Who was he?

She'd thought she recognized his voice earlier but every time she'd thought of it since, Bella doubted herself.

Was it someone she knew or was it a stranger who had become obsessed?

What had she done to even warrant that kind of obsession? Her day-to-day life since coming back to Kelby Creek had been utterly boring. When she wasn't working with her dad and Val, she was at home. When she wasn't at home, she was at a worksite. It was rare to be at neither place. Like the few times she'd gone to the bar with either Val or Justin, the one or two times she grabbed dinner with a friend from high school, or like the day she met Marco when she was supposed to be heading to accept a small business award.

If the masked man had been the one sending messages to her for more than six months, then why had he waited? Why had he waited to grab her, to attack, when for the first time in a long while, her life had actually become interesting?

Like a shot of lightning coming down from the heavens and striking her bed, adrenaline went through Bella so hard she sat up. The covers came off next as she kicked her feet over the edge of the bed. She skipped putting on her slippers, completely forgot to grab her robe and hurried out to the hallway as quickly and quietly as she could. This time she didn't feel like a teenager spying on a boy she might or might not like. This time she was a woman, afraid yet thinking about the details for what felt like the first time.

Bella put her ear to the door and tapped it lightly.

Marco's deep voice managed to be quiet yet fill her at the same time as he said, "Come in."

A look of alarm passed over his face at the sight of her. He was sitting up in the bed, a notebook and pen on his lap, and nothing but a bare chest with the bandage above the covers. She was glad she hadn't woken him.

Instead of being cute or clever, Bella got straight to the point.

"The day I met you, when I was broken down on the side of the road, he was trying to take me then, wasn't he? The man with the mask. That's why there was water in my gas tank and that's why I broke down in the middle of nowhere. He was trying to take me then."

Marco didn't try to sugarcoat it. He didn't try to give her a pep talk or even one of reassurance. Instead he nodded.

"I think so," he said. "But the thing that concerns me more is I think since then he's been practicing to do it again."

Chapter Twelve

Marco laid the notebook down on the quilt top. Bella joined him, sitting just on the other side of it so she could face him. A part of him was still hyperfocused on the case, the masked man and trying to figure out who exactly he was. Yet Marco might've gone through a lot that day but he sure wasn't dead. Which meant there was no way he wasn't going to take a moment to marvel at how beautiful the woman now in bed with him looked.

Bella's hair was soft and hung against her bare shoulders, skimming the tops of the very small straps keeping her nightshirt up. Her shorts didn't match but they did show off legs that had curve, freckles and smoothness. Since the car accident, her makeup had been washed off but that didn't subtract anything from the woman. In fact it almost added a warmth, a feeling of being comfortable that made him feel like he in a way had earned enough of her trust to be shown a version of her with her guard down.

And then there were her lips.

Ones he now knew felt every bit as great as he'd thought they would feel.

Now those lips were downturned. Her crystal blue eyes, magnetic in nature to him, scanning the paper he'd been jotting his notes on. When they traveled back up to his own, he knew that his attraction for Bella Greene was going to have to take a back seat if he was going to help keep her safe.

"After we met that first day and up until the night we ran into each other at the bar, the department had responded to several calls about cars breaking down and people being stranded," Marco started. "When I was thinking about it in the bar before I saw you, I realized that I hadn't actually asked what was wrong with the truck. I thought it was kind of strange that all of these vehicles were having problems so close together."

"Water in the gas tank," Bella guessed.

He nodded.

"One car couldn't even start and was blocking a parking lot entrance. That one had too much water in the tank. When you get over a certain amount, it basically kills the engine. There was another car that made it a little bit before it shut down. The tow truck operator who showed up used to be a mechanic and gave the car a once-over before hooking it up. His best guess without really getting into it was that there was sugar in the gas lines and tank. But I didn't pick up on the pattern right away because in between those two were two other vehicles that had broken down for unrelated reasons. One had a transmission that went kaput. The other had a hole on the inside of their tire that took us way too long to actually find. For us, it really just seemed like a series of bad luck and random people until I saw you. Then it started to bother me."

"You think that the masked man was behind all of these?" Bella readjusted where she was sitting, clearly becoming uncomfortable at the thought.

"If he's been sending you messages for almost seven months and only tried to take you this past month, then that means there's a reason he hasn't come for you before." He tried to choose his words carefully. There were only so many delicate ways he could talk about an obsessive stalker with devious intentions. Still, he didn't like what he was about to say. "I think he's trying to come up with a plan that gets you without getting him caught. I think the reason why your truck had water in its gas tank twice was because he was looking for a way to delay you from going wherever you were going. He wanted you to be able to leave your house or work or wherever you were and get caught out by yourself so he could approach you. So he could take you. I think the water in the gas tank worked but not how he wanted it to. Maybe it took too long to go into effect, maybe it happened too fast, but I think after that, after I interrupted and potentially messed up his plans, I think he played around with different methods to make it fit what he wanted."

"But there was water in my gas tank again," she pointed out. "He went back to the first thing he tried."

"That's the other thing," Marco said. "I don't think he planned on doing any of what he did today. I don't think it was his intention to put you in danger, attack me and then try to take you."

"Why do you think that?"

Marco shifted, lifted the covers enough to where she could see the very top part of the bruise that ran along his side.

"Because he would've killed me the night before when I was out running had I not heard the car and jumped out of the way at the last second. I think he would've run me down again if I hadn't managed to make it to the woods."

"He wants you out of the way. Because of me. He's targeting you."

It was something that they hadn't directly talked about since the accident but Marco knew others had discussed it. It was one of the first things Detective Lovett had pointed out when he'd come in to check on Marco at the hospital.

"I think that whoever this is doesn't like you spending time with me and when he put that message in your house, on your bathroom mirror, I don't think he imagined you'd come to me for help. Especially not to the hospital."

"So you're thinking that he acted on— what?—emotion? That he decided to move up his original plan because he was mad?"

"Jealous," Marco corrected. "You're the object of his obsession so to him my presence might be his biggest threat in his mind. Which made him impulsive. It made him sloppy." It wasn't the time but it was absolutely the emotion. Marco smirked.

Instead of getting upset at it, Bella's eyebrows went up and she mirrored the look.

"It's when people like this get sloppy that people like me get them." He put his finger down on the words that he had circled right before she'd come in. Marco waited for her to read them out loud.

"Hospital parking lot security camera."

"Hospital parking lot security camera," he repeated with a flare.

"He had to put water in my tank in the hospital parking lot," she realized.

"And since he was impulsive with how he tried to take you, then maybe he was impulsive with how he tried to sabotage your truck."

"He could have gotten sloppy there too."

Marco nodded.

"Which means we might know by tomorrow morning exactly who this guy really is."

WHEN BELLA WOKE up the next morning, she was a little confused and a lot disoriented. It took her a moment to realize that she wasn't in her own bed, in her own house. Then, slowly, she remembered whose house she was in and where in that house she had fallen asleep. It was *not* her old childhood room, that was for sure.

Instead Bella woke up in the bed meant for Marco, sans the deputy himself.

Once that memory unblurred from sleep, Bella sat up like she been shocked again by that same lightning from the night before.

With a haze over her eyes, she quickly looked at the space next to her. That part of the bed was still made from the night before. There was no Marco there, above or below the sheets.

"He slept on the couch, by the way." Bella

yelped and turned toward the bedroom doorway. Val had a coffee cup in his hand and a smug look on his face. He nodded to the love seat at the end of the bed. "I caught him coming out earlier and he told me y'all had been talking about the case and you'd fallen asleep when he had to take a call. Even though your room is four steps that way."

Val gave her a cheeky smile.

Bella rolled her eyes.

"Next time you get a crazy stalker trying to take you, then we'll see how badly you want to sleep alone."

Val's smugness wiped away. Then it was the protective brother.

"I overheard Marco and his friend the deputy talking earlier," he said. "Apparently they're looking at a lot of different leads, which I think is good, but so far haven't found anything new. They haven't found him."

That was and wasn't what Bella had wanted to hear. The idea of someone practicing for her abduction had added a new layer of fear. It was why she'd asked Marco if she could stay in the room while he mulled over some things and took a quick call from Deputy Park. The masked man had managed to make the one place in all the world where she felt the safest into somewhere she was now afraid to be alone.

She hated it.

Just like she hated that the man hadn't been caught despite being impulsive.

"Where is he now? Marco, I mean."

"Downstairs on the phone the last I saw. I think he's talking to his sister. Or at least someone he's very comfortable rolling his eyes at." Val gave her a knowing look. "I know personally I'm very comfortable with showing my sister just how much she annoys me. Which is quite frequent."

Bella grabbed the pillow next to her and threw it at the door. Val dodged it, laughing, and left.

By the time she got ready and made it downstairs, her family and Marco were together in the dining room, talking. Her mother squeezed her shoulder, her very own form of good-morning, and handed her a cup of coffee. Bella took a seat next to Marco, who remained in conversation with her father. It took her a few sips before she realized that they were talking about her stalker.

"Wait, I thought you said no one had been caught?" she asked, directing her question to Val.

He shook his head but it was Marco who answered. Being so close to him, she could smell his aftershave and noted that the stubble along his jaw was gone.

"They haven't been. Detective Lovett is still manning the search but your dad pointed out that we haven't had a chance to see how your house was broken into." He passed her the plate of muffins her mother had no doubt stress-cooked earlier that morning. "After we were attacked, no one went over there to see if they could figure out how he got in to leave the message. So, since the department is short-staffed and currently on a manhunt for this guy and, according to the sheriff, I'm not coming back in today to work, I thought I could check it out. Maybe find a clue that could help."

A feeling of equal parts excitement and nerves pulsed through Bella.

"I would personally love to figure out how he got in too," she said. "The only people who have keys to my house are in this room. I don't even have a spare one hidden outside just in case I get locked out."

Marco nodded like he was mentally taking notes. Bella knew that part of being a deputy was thinking on your feet and problem-solving but the more she looked at him, she was starting to see the makings of a detective. She decided later on, maybe when life calmed down, she would ask if he had any aspirations to try to become one. Until then she was thankful for every inclination he had and acted on to help her get to the bottom of what was happening.

"Okay, well, you give me your key and I'll head out in a few minutes once Carlos is here and I can have a chance to talk to him and see if we can get someone else out here."

Bella didn't realize that she was shaking her head until her father made a noise at her.

"You're not going alone," she interjected.

"And you're not coming," Marco was fast to reply.

"It's my house. You can't tell me I can't come. Plus, I know it better than anyone. If there's something out of place, if there's something wrong, I'm the only one here who has the best chance of seeing that."

"If this masked man has come after you in the daylight and in the company of a law enforcement officer and in such a brazen attack, then going home to a place where we know he's been inside isn't the best idea," Marco said.

He was getting feisty. That was the only word Bella could think of for it. It was as if he were as excited as a child jumping up and down because he was next in line to see Santa.

Marco wanted to help. He wanted to solve this and he wanted to do it now.

Still, she shook her head. This time her father

spoke up but before he could make his own argument Bella firmly planted hers.

"I am no more safe here than I would be there," she stated. "But at least there I have a chance to find something that might be able to help us stop this guy from ever coming for me again and hurting any of y'all who get in his way. I'm going." She looked Marco square in the face. "The only choice you get to make now is if *you* want to come with *me.*"

Marco chewed on that for a moment. Her family remained quiet. She thought she was about to have to make a second argument, maybe throw in a few minutes of her raised I'm-serious voice that she used on suppliers who tried to overcharge Greene Thumb and Hammer, but finally Marco caved.

And he did so with a smile that put heat into her veins.

"Yes, ma'am."

Chapter Thirteen

Watching Bella convince her family that they couldn't come with her, Marco and Carlos was like watching a master class in persuasion. She managed to shift paternal and maternal worry enough so that they now believed they'd help more by staying away. Though maybe it did help that her father seemed to genuinely trust Marco.

Grant had pulled him aside before they left with Carlos and had quietly told him in no uncertain terms that he protected her the first time and he expected even better results the second time around. If there was a second time. He was of the same thought with Marco that the masked man, if he had any sense, was long gone from Kelby Creek. Or at least in such deep hiding that he wasn't going to chance another attempt at getting her.

"You told me your story," Grant had added. "I know your résumé from your last job now.

Which means I know you're good. I need you to stay good. You hear me?"

"I hear you."

Now Bella was standing on the front porch of her own home, peeking in through the windows, trying to figure out if it was safe for her to come in. At all times Marco kept his eyes on her while moving from room to room at the front part of the house while Carlos swept everything else.

It was then, standing on a rug that had more personality than most people Marco had met, that he started to suspect not only did he like Deputy Park but he was also starting to trust him.

"Unless you have some kind of hidden compartment or underground bunker, there's no one in this house but us," Carlos concluded when they all converged on the front porch again.

The tension that had been building in Bella's shoulders on the ride over lessened but didn't entirely drop.

"All right," she said, turning to Marco with nothing but focus. "Let's see if I can't supersleuth us a clue."

Marco trailed behind Bella while Carlos stayed outside. They went from room to room, as she inspected everything in silence. Marco was almost ashamed to say his attention kept splitting from the woman to what the woman had built around her.

Before then Marco had formed an opinion about Bella Greene. If he'd been asked about what she was like before entering her home, he would've said that the one word he would use to describe her was *surprising.* Then he would have probably followed that up with *loud,* but not loud in a bad way. She knew what she wanted, she said what she wanted and she wouldn't stand by and let someone else tell her what she wanted. After spending time at her family's home the night before, Marco would've added that he believed that Bella fiercely loved her family, just as they fiercely loved her back. But going through her home? Marco found a new word to describe the woman.

Warm.

It wasn't a poetic description, and it certainly wasn't original, but the more he saw of her private life, the more he felt warm just by being there.

The house was older, tidy, but also messy exactly where it counted. There were magazines on the coffee table, straightened and obviously for guests, but then there was an empty coffee cup with lipstick on the brim and different colors of nail polish resting on a coupon for take-out. Marco could almost imagine Bella sitting on the couch, watching TV and trying to do her nails at the same time. He even spotted a smear of purple paint with glitter against the table. He bet she'd missed with the applicator and had left it, admitting defeat about ever getting it off the wood without hurting the finish.

From there Marco fell into unintentionally comparing Bella to his last girlfriend. She'd been obsessed with plants. She had potted everything you could think of, sitting on or hanging from almost every available space in her apartment. Bella was in no way the same. There wasn't a living plant in any room of the house. But fake succulents and cacti? She had those in spades. The thought of her getting fake plants instead of real ones almost made Marco chuckle to himself. Green Thumb and Hammer worked on landscaping as well as building structures and yet Bella was 100 percent fake plants. He could just imagine her complaining about how she didn't want to take her work home.

There were other details throughout the house too. Subtle and not-so-subtle. Details that told a story about the woman who lived there. Framed photos across all the walls, just like at her parents'. Family and friends and adventures between them all. There were books strewn around on how to knit tiny gnomes and how to cook quiche in tiny iron skillets. A small closet filled with costumes presumably for Halloween and a small office that was still being renovated but housed a small plastic trophy that said World's Best Daughter.

There was personality in the house.

And it was warm.

For a moment, after seeing the colorful quilt on her bed, the empty wineglass on her nightstand and one stuffed bear wearing a construction hat sitting on the chair in the corner, Marco forgot why they were there.

All he knew was that he wanted to stay.

"I have no idea how he got in," Bella said, throwing her arms up in defeat. "I know this place inch for inch and yet I'm not seeing anything that sends up red flags."

She motioned to the windows.

"Every window is locked and can only be opened from the inside," she continued. "There's no broken glass or broken doors anywhere. I unlock and lock every door I walk through that leads from the outside to inside and—"

Marco went from feeling warm to startled by his own interrupting thought. He reached out and grabbed her elbow, stopping her midsentence.

"That's it. Jennifer Parkridge."

Bella's eyebrow slid up.

"Jennifer Parkridge?" she repeated. Before he

could explain, that look of excitement of something clicking into place came over her. "Her house... But that could be a coincidence, surely."

Marco felt like he was onto something he should have seen already.

"She had a broken door and nothing taken. You don't have any broken doors and a message was left behind. If the masked man has been making a plan to take you at a specific time and in a specific place, who's to say that it's not just cars he's been practicing with?"

"I don't know. That's kind of a stretch, don't you think? All the bad that's been happening in Kelby Creek the last six to seven months can't be because of him. Can it?"

Marco could feel it in his gut, just like the night at the bar when he had first seen Bella and Justin. He knew something was up about the cars and yet he had pushed it to the back burner. That error in judgment, that lack of hustle to get to the bottom of his feeling, had almost cost Bella and him their lives.

He wasn't going to make the same mistake now.

"I think it's time we head back to the sheriff's department."

BELLA WAS SURPRISED at how big the file was. Or really how thick. Its pages nearly covered the meeting room's tabletop after Marco spread them all out.

"This is just in the last six months?" she asked. "These are all transcripts of people calling in?"

"They're calls that we responded to," he corrected, eyes down and scanning the current paper he was standing over. "The department, I mean. I physically didn't go to all these."

Bella whistled and she side-eyed the door. It was closed.

"And you're sure it's okay for us to be doing this?"

Marco wasn't as quick to answer that one. When he did, he added in a shrug.

"We're trying to help stop a stalker, which can only help the town, which can only help the department. So *really* we're not actually looking at papers we're not supposed to, we are just helping in a way that we need to be discreet about. Besides, most of these are public records, and since I'm guarding you, it's just more efficient to do this together."

Bella couldn't help it. She chuckled.

"*Wow*, if that wasn't some fancy footwork around a good ole *no, we shouldn't be doing this*."

Marco shrugged.

"If you'd rather me say we're being fluid with

the law to get to where we need to be to *help* the law, would that be better?"

Bella returned her gaze to her own stack of papers.

"You know it wouldn't, but, hey, you were cute when you said it so I'll let it slide."

She hadn't meant to say *cute* out loud, but just like she let his stepping around the truth go, he let her schoolgirl description of him lie. The meeting room became quiet again just as it had been off and on for almost half an hour since they'd gotten there. A few minutes later and that silence was broken.

"There have been three break-ins in the past six months including Jennifer Parkridge's house," Marco said, putting his hands on his hips. "While each happened differently, aside from Jennifer, the intruders were caught and both are currently in prison for previous offenses. As for anything else that might be suspicious or look like someone acting out parts of a plan to abduct someone, I'm not finding anything that jumps out at me."

Bella didn't want to but she said the same for her section of papers.

"The only thing I really found is that there are still a few people in Kelby Creek who aren't exactly fans of the department." She tapped a paper that was near her. "Like someone continuously messing with the department's breaker."

Bella dropped back into the chair that was next to her. She let out a hefty sigh. This search was starting to wear away at her will to live, buried among the complaints and police reports from the residents of Kelby Creek. Marco followed suit. He took the chair opposite her and shook his head.

"Whoever the masked man is, he knows you," he started. "Which means there's a good possibility you *actually* know him. You said he sounded familiar when he called for you at the storage facility, right?"

Bella nodded.

"Familiar but I couldn't place it. Just that I *know* it. And, believe me, I've been trying."

"So maybe it's someone that you had contact with in the past six to seven months. When it first started." He leaned forward on the table and made a temple with his hands on its top. His eyes latched on to hers and Bella knew she couldn't look away even if she wanted to. And she didn't. "I know we've already been over this, but can you think of anyone who might have shown that strong of interest in you? Maybe an ex-boyfriend or someone you dated?"

Bella didn't look away but she did squirm a little. It was slightly embarrassing. Like her social life since coming back to Kelby Creek, her dating life hadn't been that great. Her last ex had called her too intimidating. The one before that had called her annoying. He'd been easy to break up with.

"The last guy I was serious with lives in Florida now with his wife and newborn baby. And before you ask if I'm sure, let me just tell you that I stalked his social media profiles last night to make sure. There were a ton of tagged pictures of him and his family at some little kid's birthday party at a Chuck E. Cheese around the time we were attacked. My ex *before* that was someone I dated two years ago. The last I heard he was in Germany as a contractor with *his* family." She shook her head. "Neither one of them showed that much interest in me when we were dating, so I can't imagine they'd be coming for me after the fact. I doubt they'd even have the time."

Thankfully Marco didn't seem to focus on the news that Bella had only dated two men in the last few years. Not that that was particularly a bad thing, but for her it wasn't something that she liked to lead with in a conversation.

"Okay, so let's guess that it's not someone that you've been in a relationship with, but is there anyone you dated in the last year? Someone you weren't exactly serious about but went out with?"

Bella started to laugh, mostly because once again, she was about to point out that her social life and her romantic life hadn't been that impressive in the past. But then she remembered something.

Marco must have realized it.

"What?" He leaned forward with rapt attention.

"I *did* go out with a guy, about maybe seven or eight months ago. I don't really count him since I didn't actually stay the entire dinner."

"What's his name?" Marco reached for a piece of paper and pen.

"If you believe it, Conrad Abernethy."

Marco looked up at that.

"And you're sure he wasn't using a fake name?"

She laughed.

"Yeah, his name was Conrad Abernethy. From what I was told, he almost became a Conrad Abernethy the Third but his mother took pity on him."

"He lives in Kelby Creek?"

Bella nodded.

"I don't know where exactly but I met him at the Rosewater Bar. He was nice, cute and made pleasant conversation when we first met so when he asked me out I said yes. We went for dinner, I think two nights later, but I didn't stay all the way through it."

"Why not?"

"From the moment I sat down, he talked about himself nonstop and then the one time I tried to add something to the conversation, he did not respond in the way that I thought he should have. I texted a friend to come get me, which I have never done before, and made an excuse to leave before we'd even finished our meal."

Marco's eyebrow had slid up in question.

"What did he say that you didn't like?"

Bella felt the heat lift from the embarrassment whirling in her stomach and pool in her cheeks. She cleared her throat.

"Conrad told me during his one-man soliloquy that he was a taste entrepreneur. And, before you ask if you heard me right, just know that you did. Conrad was a self-proclaimed taster of all things alcohol. He was telling me a story about how he traveled the world tasting all these different drinks one summer in between his freshman and sophomore years of college. He told me that before he had gone off on this trip that he'd had a six-pack of abs. But when he came back, he'd had so much to drink that those six-pack abs had become more of a keg.

So, me trying to be funny, I said that before *I* went to college I also had a six-pack but now all I had were two jugs." She motioned to her chest, now fully immersed in embarrassment.

Thankfully Marco burst out laughing.

"See?" she exclaimed. "That's the reaction I was hoping to get! It was a joke after all! But no. He stared at me like I'd just insulted his very soul. Not only did he not laugh, he didn't say anything and let us fall into this really weird tension-filled silence. I had to break it myself and I think what I said was something along the lines of *man I really hope they come by with breadsticks soon!*"

Marco was still laughing.

"That's when you texted your friend to come get you?"

Bella nodded, relieved that the story was over.

"He even told me he had better things to do when I made an excuse about Dad having an emergency," she added. "He didn't try to re-schedule and he never texted or called. I haven't seen him since then. I'm not even sure he lives in Kelby Creek now."

Marco's laughter had died away. He was back to work-mode.

"You can never tell what someone is capable of until they do it." He took the paper and stood up. "This Conrad may be full of himself and he may not be able to take a good joke but that doesn't mean he couldn't be the one who has been after you. For all—"

Bella sat up, ramrod straight.

"I'm an idiot," she interrupted. Adrenaline had burst through her as a memory dislodged. She found Marco's gaze again and shook her head. "You remember how I said that *hello there, friend* was kind of like my catchphrase during and after college?"

"Yeah?"

"Well, it also kind of became how I greeted people when I was nervous."

Marco caught on quick. She could tell by how the muscle in his jaw twitched and his eyes narrowed. A bloodhound catching on to a scent.

"And did you greet Conrad like that when you first met him at the bar?"

Bella's mind was flashing through the memories of the first night she met him. She wasn't sure if she would have remembered it otherwise but now she did.

"Yes. I was so awkward with it. After he introduced himself, I said, *Hello there, friend. I'm Bella Greene.*"

Chapter Fourteen

Conrad Abernethy was technically a local yet no one could agree on the last time anyone had seen him.

His employer at a production factory in the city hadn't seen him in weeks. His neighbor hadn't seen him in days. The bartender at the Rosewater Bar hadn't seen him in months. When Marco called his last-known number, it went straight to voice mail.

It was more than enough to pique his interest, if only to rule out the young man.

"I don't know how you are at reading women, but she was really mad at you back there." Carlos came around the side of his patrol car and kept his voice low. "I mean, for a second there, I thought she was about to go for my gun and make us take her with us."

Carlos was joking but, then again, they both realized that wasn't exactly true. Telling Bella that she couldn't come with them to talk to Conrad had been a harder fight than Marco had imagined.

"I'm in this more than you," she had said, frustration punctuating every word. "And didn't you also say you think the masked man would be long gone by now?"

"Or in hiding," he'd pointed out. "And if it is Conrad, and he is in hiding, then what better place to hunker down than his own home?"

After that it was a volley of back-and-forths until Detective Lovett and his fiancée came in. Millie must have sensed that Bella needed to vent and to someone preferably not in law enforcement. They went into the detective's office while Marco updated Foster on their small-but-still-there lead.

"Let me know if you find anything. I'm about to finish off a few of my own from yesterday."

Carlos had been more than eager to get to the bottom of who the stalker was and, surprisingly, not just because it was the right thing to do. He'd been candid during the car ride to Conrad's house.

"I don't think it's right that you go through what you did at your old department only to come here to ours and be nearly killed by a guy with a Halloween-mask fetish," he'd said. "I know things that aren't fair happen to a lot of people and that in itself is not fair but still, definitely not cool."

Marco had stiffened at the mention of his last job. Not that he had been in denial about everyone else in the department not knowing about his past. Civilians being oblivious made sense. What had happened had nothing to do with anyone other than the cop Marco had taken down.

That didn't mean he wanted to hash it out with his new partner. Though Carlos did manage to get a few more words in before they arrived at their destination.

"I know some people don't get why you did it but I just have to say I do, and I would have done the same. It's crazy you had to leave because of it."

He hadn't corrected the man.

Marco hadn't had to leave—he'd chosen to do it.

"Thanks," was all Marco had said in response.

The focus shifted off the past and onto Conrad and his future. If he was the masked man, everything was about to change.

Since Marco was technically off duty, Carlos went around back to check the perimeter while Marco went right up to the front door. Conrad lived in a house that had the creek butted up against his backyard. There was a dock in the distance and a boat anchored there but it and the house were more run-down than well-kept. The one-story was small and splintered, a shutter hung on for dear life beneath one of the front windows, and if it hadn't been a little cold, Marco was sure he'd see a lot more overgrowth and weeds around the yard. There was a detached garage to the left of the house but the metal door was closed and locked by a padlock against the concrete.

Marco couldn't tell if anyone was home but he was getting the impression that, if they were, it hadn't been for long. The home seemed largely unlived in.

Marco made sure his jacket was hiding his holstered gun so he wouldn't potentially spook the man. His badge was in his back pocket, also ready to go if needed.

He knocked on the door and realized he was holding his breath.

Nothing.

Nothing sounded on the other side of the door and no one called out.

Marco knocked again, moving to the closest window when done. The curtain was drawn. Just like all of the windows facing the road. He couldn't see in and he still couldn't hear anything.

Was Conrad not there or was he hiding?

Movement made Marco turn to the side of the house.

It was Carlos and he had his gun out.

"I think you should come see this."

Marco followed his partner around the side and up to the back porch. He slowed down considerably as he moved up the stairs. Marco pulled his gun out.

"There." Carlos pointed to the back door. It was ajar, its wood splintered around where it should have been locked.

Carlos shared a look with him. They nodded, a wordless understanding of what to do next. One stood in the doorway while the other pushed it open. Marco called out but it was Carlos who went in first.

"This is Deputy Rossi with the Dawn County Sherriff's Department. If anyone is inside, identify yourself now!" Carlos was already inside but Marco kept on. "We're coming in. If anyone is inside, let us know now!"

No one called back and nothing made a sound. Only their boots against the tile that led from the back door and into the kitchen.

But what it lacked in sound, it more than made up for with smell.

"Oh, my God."

Carlos put his freehand over his nose and

pinched. Marco threw his nose into the crook of his arm.

They didn't say it then but they'd been in law enforcement long enough to know exactly what they'd find around the corner. Or at least Marco did. He'd once done a wellness check that had turned into him calling in the coroner when he was a rookie. That smell was bad. This one was too. Marco guessed he was about to have to make a similar call to their dispatcher.

Carlos rounded the corner first. He lowered his gun just as Marco stopped at his side.

For a moment, neither one of them spoke.

"Well, I think it's safe to say we found our guy," Carlos said. "But I don't think he's going to hurt anyone anymore."

Marco lowered his own gun.

Conrad Abernethy was lying on the ground, surrounded by dried blood and eyes open and staring at the ceiling. That would have been bad enough but it was the mask on the couch behind him that had all of Marco's attention.

"THEY THINK ONE of Marco's shots landed on Conrad at the storage facility and instead of going to the hospital and chance getting caught, he went home to hide."

Bella's father shook his head. Justin did too. They made various tsking noises. Disappointed at the unnecessary loss of life and the violence that had led up to it. Bella didn't know how she felt. Was she disappointed that the man had thrown away his life for no reason? Was she relieved that it was over? Was she angry that it had started in the first place?

Bella couldn't stick to one feeling. Mainly because she hadn't had the time to process Conrad's death herself.

Or, really, with the person she wanted to process it with.

"I still can't believe any of this happened," Justin decided on after a moment. "I feel sorry for everyone involved."

They were all at her parents' house, ruminating on the news. Since Marco and Carlos had made the discovery, the threat level over Bella had ceased to exist. Which meant standing around the sheriff's department, waiting, didn't make much sense. So Justin had picked up Bella and her father, who'd not yet found his keys, and taken them both to the house. Now everyone had coffee. Everyone but Val, who was still at the site of Justin's shed-in-progress. Bella bet dollars to donuts that the gossip mill would reach him before they even headed back.

"But this means it's over, right?" Justin added. "For you, I mean."

Bella nodded, then she cringed. Caught between several emotions still.

Conrad's body wasn't the only thing Marco had found. In his brief phone conversation with her, he'd listed the other concerning items within the house. Chief among them was the Halloween mask their attacker had worn, next to Conrad's body.

That would have been enough for her to believe Conrad was her stalker but, if it hadn't been there, the trash can full of notes that read *Hello there, friend* would have done the trick.

"I'll feel better once I get all the details from Marco." She looked to her father, who, in any other instance, might chastise her for trying to skip out on work. "I was wondering if I could wait here until he's done?"

She didn't say it but Bella knew her father picked up on the reason she didn't want to stay at her house to wait.

Bella didn't want to be alone yet.

"I'm sure your mother would love the company."

He smiled and ruffled her hair as they left. Bella slid into that familial warmth and safety, and stayed there with her mother until afternoon turned to night. Then the anxiousness set in, especially when she called Marco and it went straight to voice mail.

Instead of waiting for the man to reach out to her, Bella decided their last few days warranted her reaching out to his partner.

Deputy Park was surprisingly forthcoming with information.

One minute she was wrapping banana nut bread with her mother and several minutes later, she was sitting in her mother's car outside an apartment complex, staring at number 12B.

According to Deputy Park, Marco should have just gotten inside after a long day. His emphasis on long was probably a not-so-subtle point that Marco needed rest.

Bella agreed with that sentiment; in fact she believed he deserved it more than anyone, and yet there she was, holding banana bread on a Halloween-themed plate, wearing perfume and hoping that the deputy wasn't so tired that he couldn't see her.

"Just go knock on the door, you dingbat," Bella told herself with mounting annoyance riding along with her nerves. "Worst-case, you just say thank-you, drop off the bread and go back to your parents' place to have leftover lasagna. So, just get out of the car."

Bella finally listened to herself but nearly chickened out halfway up the stairs to the second floor. Apartment 12B was a corner unit and that meant extra steps to get to it. Those extra steps were filled with an anxiety that Bella was struggling to tamp down.

She didn't like it or understand it.

She'd been around the deputy time and time again. Heck, she'd even kissed and been kissed by the man!

And that's the problem, her brain spit out just as she knocked on the door. *You want to kiss him again but this time you don't want to stop.*

Bella didn't get the chance to give a rebuttal to herself before the door opened.

If his eyes weren't so quick to lock on to her, Bella might have taken a second to let out a breath.

She'd seen the man shirtless before at the hospital and in the guest bedroom. She knew that his upper body was well-toned and was no doubt an exciting prequel to what lay below, but just because you know that water with ice in it is cold, doesn't mean you're always prepared for when it's thrown into your face. It didn't help that Marco's pants were gone, a towel in its place hanging low. It did nothing for the water droplets across his chest or the slickness of his wet hair.

"Bella." His eyes widened in surprise but he stepped back quickly and motioned her in. "Hey. Come in."

Bella felt the heat of a blush rising but went past him with a smile.

"Sorry to just drop by like this," she said in a hurry. "I was worried about you and your phone was off so I called Deputy Park and he told me where you lived and—" Bella cut herself off and whirled around to face him once the door was closed. She held out the banana bread like the racing baton at a track meet. "Mom and I made you some dessert since you, you know, saved my life and—"

This time it was Marco who interrupted.

He closed the space between them in two long strides. Bella didn't have time to move as he caught her face in his hands, leaned down and pressed his lips against hers with force.

Not that Bella would have wanted to move if she'd had the time.

Though the dessert on the plate between them couldn't take the heat. It made a loud crack as it hit the wood floor and broke.

Marco was startled at the sound.

He jumped back like she'd bitten him.

His eyes went down to the plate, then right back to hers. Bella could read his apology before he put it into words. So she thought it prudent to stop him and set him straight first.

"It's okay. I promise I've always hated that plate."

That was all it took. Marco closed the space between them again and pulled Bella into an embrace that made her tingle from head to toe.

Had she known those were the magic words to get Marco Rossi to kiss her again, she would have broken the plate herself.

Chapter Fifteen

The road to hell is paved with good intentions.
The path to Marco's bed was paved with desire,
surprise and the faint smell of banana lingering
between them.

Marco's hands were tangling in Bella's hair,
pulling her lips against his without much breathing in between. She'd already made a noise
against his lips, a moan. It was enough to make
the voice inside his head, telling Marco to calm
down, go absolutely quiet.

He'd spent the entire day dealing with the
aftermath of finding Conrad Abernethy's body.
The sheriff started off the official aspects of it
when he showed up at Conrad's house and reminded Marco that he wasn't supposed to be
there. That he was off duty and supposed to be
resting. But just as Marco was about to rally up
a response that would keep him firmly tied to
the case, Sheriff Chamblin relented with a grin.

"This was good work," he'd said. "Another

reason why I'm really glad you decided to come to Dawn County."

Marco had good reason to not be a fan of authority despite actually being a part of authority. Yet he became a fan of the sheriff that day. Not only had he allowed Marco to stay at the scene, he'd okayed him and Carlos to stick around Detective Lovett as he did his investigation. Together the three of them had been painfully thorough going through Conrad's house. The only break Marco had taken was to call Bella and let her know that Conrad would no longer be stalking her. That he would no longer be a threat to her or her family ever again.

What happened after that became a blur of cataloging evidence, talking to several people that Conrad's death would directly affect and, his least favorite, paperwork.

In between that paperwork and coming home, his phone had died just as his thoughts became consumed with everything that had happened. He needed to let go, he knew that, but during his shower he couldn't focus on anything else.

Not calling his sister or parents to let them know that the threat was gone. Not notifying Carlos to let him know that he was no longer at work but would be coming in the next day. Not even reaching out to Bella, who was starting to become an almost every-moment thought in his head.

Something felt unfinished to Marco but he didn't know what or why and that something had been bothering him when he'd heard the knock at his front door.

Seeing Bella had been a shock to his system that had quickly turned to fire in his veins. Seeing her standing there, face deepening into the shade of crimson, and with a Halloween platter holding dessert, something inside Marco changed.

All at once and yet, not.

He hadn't planned on kissing her and he decided against planning to stop. And, unless he was missing the mark, Bella seemed to be on the same page.

While his hands ran through her hair and then down to the small of her back, hers roamed the space across his bare chest and up over his shoulders. They explored the back of his neck, then up into his hair. Then they went rogue, traveling everywhere.

Her lips were hot against his, her body too. He could feel the heat through her blouse.

It made him want her more.

They seemed again to be on the same page.

At the edge of his bed, she took her own shirt off and threw it across the room like she was playing a carnival game and gunning for the top prize. It was such an abrupt movement that Marco actually paused to laugh.

"What?" Bella's voice was low and smoldering. The towel around his waist was becoming tighter by the second.

"Nothing. Nothing at all."

Even to his ears, his voice had dropped to gravel and a growl.

After that, there was no space between them until both were on top of his bed. Somewhere between the floor and the covers, Bella had lost another article of clothing.

Marco ran his hand down the curve of her breast before hooking his thumb around her nipple. She let out a little gasp as he replaced his hand with his tongue.

"Holy macaroni," she breathed.

Marco hadn't heard that one before but he found it oddly endearing.

He moved his mouth up to her collarbone before dancing the line of her neck to her jaw. There he kissed up to her ear and whispered once more with the voice that let her know exactly what it was that he wanted even if he didn't say the exact words.

"I never got to ask, if you decided that you'd jumped the gun with me or not."

Bella's lips were parted. She was breathing heavily, not a pant but definitely not steady.

"If you're asking if I've decided if I like you, Deputy Rossi, I can assure you I don't make banana bread for just anyone."

Those lips, those perfect lips, curved up at the corners.

Bella Greene was being cheeky.

And Marco was loving every second of it.

THE TOWEL CAME off with unsurprising speed. Mostly because Bella was the one who freed the deputy from it. After that, there was no more banter or teasing. It was just two people who had been fighting an attraction finally giving in. Finally being free.

At least, that's what it felt like to Bella. Logically she knew that she and Marco hadn't known each other long. That she didn't know his middle name or even his mother's name and if you asked her what his favorite color or his favorite movie was, she'd have had to shrug. But life was weird and timing was even stranger. Because, even though she knew she didn't really know the man, Bella couldn't help but feel like he was it.

He was the reason why she hadn't been that interested in her dating life since coming to Kelby Creek.

It felt like a part of her had been waiting.

Waiting for Marco to come to town.

It was a significant thought that popped into Bella's head as the two of them collided beneath the sheets, but it was one that was still there two hours later as they tucked back into bed after their shower. Something that was also very stimulating.

Bella's head was resting against Marco's bare chest, her arm carefully thrown over his stomach, and she was vaguely aware of the sound of the heat turning on and blowing through the vents above. She'd helped rebandage his stitches and had finally been able to take a closer look at the bruising and now-healing cuts he'd gotten from the attacks. Even though she was looking at the ceiling, she knew she was near a particularly nasty cut that had very narrowly missed needing stitches.

It was all the reminder needed to pull a sigh from her.

The arm Marco had around her shifted, and his thumb rubbed her back.

"What's wrong?" His voice brushed against the darkness around them. Moonlight, streaming through a crack in the blinds over the window across from the bed, provided the only illumination in the room. Instead of being afraid as she had been at her parents' house at the thought of being in the darkness alone, now she felt oddly content. No doubt because of the man wrapped around her.

Still, all the good in the world couldn't chip away the idea of Conrad Abernethy and his obsession that had led to his own death.

"What's right?" The question slipped out of her mouth before she could stop it.

Marco continued to rub her back.

"I happen to think this feels pretty right," he said, tone light. "And I *really* enjoyed how right it felt to do what we did earlier in this very bed and then in the shower." She felt him shrug. "But that could just be me."

Bella let out a small but true laugh.

Then it all went away. She could no longer keep herself from talking about the one thing she had told herself she wouldn't when she had been headed to Marco's in the first place.

"I'm sorry you had to shoot him," she said. "I can't imagine how hard that is and, I just wanted to let you know that I'm here if you want to talk about it. Anytime."

Bella thought she had messed up. Marco stiffened. But then, slowly, that tension let out. His voice was soft as he responded, though he caught her off guard with what he said.

"Can I ask you a question? One that might sound a bit pointless now?"

Bella nodded against him.

"Sure. Anything."

"Do you know why your dad decided to trust me? I mean, did he tell you why, because I got the impression he doesn't do that with everyone."

"He doesn't," she said, sure in her words. "For my dad, trust can only ever be earned. It's never something that's given. So, I guess in the hospital you must've earned that trust. Though, I have to point out, you did also save his favorite child."

She meant for him to laugh or do that quick chuckle that she was becoming accustomed to. The one that felt like a bad boy still trying to be bad despite being humored by a woman a full foot shorter than him.

He didn't.

He was sticking to her father and the trust he'd earned.

"I told him something," he went on to say. "In the hospital. I told him the story of why I came to Kelby Creek, of all places, and I don't understand why that was enough to earn anything, especially trust."

Bella switched her focus to avoiding tensing. She wondered why her father had been so quick to get on Team Rossi but hadn't asked him. Just like she hadn't asked Marco what had happened that made him decide to become the law in a town that couldn't help but look down on those in charge.

But now that he was on the cusp of potentially telling her, Bella hoped he would shed the rest of his armor and trust her with the answer.

To her utter surprise, he continued talking.

And he gave her more than she could've hoped for.

"What I didn't tell your dad was something that I've already touched on with you a little bit," he started. "See, my biological parents were really young when they got pregnant with me and then they were still young when they got pregnant with Amy. That in itself wouldn't have been necessarily an issue but my mother was killed in a mugging shortly after Amy was born, and my father couldn't handle that. He took us to his mother's house and then left and never came back. My grandmother tried to take care of us but had never really wanted to be a mom in the first place. That went double for a grandmother taking care of her two small grandchildren. That's how we entered foster care two years after we were dropped off."

Marco didn't pause or hesitate. It was like he was reading a teleprompter or saying something that he'd rehearsed. It made Bella's heart ache even more at how detached he sounded from it.

She couldn't help but hold him a little bit tighter as he continued.

"We got lucky and were adopted pretty quickly. They're very loving parents and since they got us so young, they're really all we know. A lot of the time, I know 'specially for Amy, we forget that we aren't biologically theirs. But, sometimes, there are these moments where all I can see are the cracks that had to be created for us to fall through to get to them."

He sighed. Bella waited.

"Originally I thought I joined law enforcement because I had always felt protective of my sister and wanted to keep her safe, even when we were little. I felt an almost peace in that. But then I realized that the real reason I wanted to be an officer or deputy was because of what happened to my biological mom. In my head, I knew there was nothing I could have done to save her, not even the remote possibility, considering I was a toddler. But I guess in my heart, I always felt that if I couldn't save her, then the least I could do was save someone else."

He let out another breath. It was long and low. Bella doubted even if the lights were on that she would have been able to read whatever emotion was currently resting in his expression. The best thing she could do for him in that moment was to stay still and listen.

So she did, her own heart in a vise.

"Because we were lucky enough to have such great adoptive parents and, honestly, a great childhood, Amy and I became big believers in the idea of choosing your family, instead of just being born into it," he continued. "When I became a deputy at the sheriff's department at my last job, I didn't mean to do it but I chose everyone there as my family."

This time tension ringed Marco's body. No hint of relaxing came with it.

"There was one guy in particular that, in hindsight, I realize I might have looked up to as a father figure. He was my mentor when I first got there and, because of staffing issues, actually became my partner for a while." Bella felt him shake his head, as if disapproving of his past self's actions. "I didn't see it at first. I should have, but I just didn't. You know how they say you can only ever be betrayed by your friends? Well, it was a hard truth that I learned very quickly when I caught him planting evidence on one of the town's repeat offenders."

The way he said it, the clear pain and anger in it, made Bella shift so she could stare up at his profile. He was looking up at the ceiling but she knew all he was seeing was the past.

"He was quick to remind me that this guy was a nobody and that this way we could get him out of our hair for good. But that didn't work for me and so the guy who was supposed to have my back tried to use that friendship as a reason not to turn him in. I *owed* him. But I didn't listen. Instead I marched right up to the sheriff's office and told him everything." That anger came out again, moving through the end of his sentence like a snake hiding in the tall grass and waiting to pounce. "I'd been there for three years, *three* years of hard work, dedication and absolute loyalty. And not just with any one person but with the entire department. They were family. I trusted them. But they didn't trust me."

Bella had to say something then, partly because she herself was starting to get angry too. Marco had already done so much for her and it had only been a few weeks since they met. Having him around for three years? She couldn't imagine not believing in him completely.

"What do you mean they didn't trust you?" she asked, hotly. "They thought you were lying?"

Marco shrugged.

"My partner managed to convince them that I was trying to pit cop against cop in some weird power trip and everyone jumped on the bandwagon. Then, when I brought up the hard evidence I had against him, no one said a word until the sheriff offered me a deal to save face for the department. He would make my partner retire early, I would get a promotion and no one would have to know outside of the department what had happened if I just dropped everything."

"I can assume by you being here that you didn't take that deal."

Marco shook his head.

"I made it public so it would warrant an investigation. The sheriff took heat, lost his re-election, and all the people who were so quick to not trust me decided that I was still in the wrong. I even had one guy tell me that you don't stab family in the back, to which I replied they weren't my family after all. A week later, I decided to apply for a job here, in Kelby Creek. In my mind, if I was going to have to work for redemption, then I should at least do it somewhere people worthy of that redemption were. That's why I'm here. And *that* is what I told your father."

Bella's body was sore. From a myriad of things that went from pain to pleasure, but she wasted no time sitting up to look at the man still holding her.

Even in the darkness, his eyes were easy to see.

They locked on to her gaze and waited.

Bella smiled.

"If you're asking, without asking, why my father decided to trust you based on that story, I can tell you exactly why and even use an example I've heard him use before." She placed her hand gently on his chest, his heart beat thumping against her palm. She hoped he heard her, *really* heard her, and the pride that went behind her words. "You walked into someone's house that was on fire and you tried to help them and you got burned. Then instead of never ever risking that pain again, you walked into another burning building, trying to help those who might be inside."

She shrugged, knowing it was not a pretty or completely accurate analogy but she still brought it home, just as she'd heard her father do before when talking about trust.

"The people who earn trust are those who deserve trust. And those who try to help people by being selfless and asking for nothing in return but the common courtesy of being decent? Well, that's a slam dunk in my father's book. Just as it is in mine. I trust you because you're worth trusting."

Bella lowered her head to his and kissed Marco for all she was worth. When she pulled away, her lips were still tingling. Had someone not started banging on the apartment's front door, Bella was sure that kiss would've continued.

But someone did and that was all Marco needed to become her protector all over again.

Chapter Sixteen

When danger struck and the woman you were falling for was with you, there wasn't any time for a wardrobe change.

Marco was out of bed in nothing but his boxers and to his gun in a flash.

"Stay here."

Bella wrapped the covers around her and didn't listen. Marco made sure he was at the door first, Bella securely behind him. His weapon was low, his shirt and pants were back in his room, and he sounded ready to fight when he called out.

"Who is it?"

There was an immediate answer back.

"Marco?" It was a woman's voice. "Let me in! It's cold out here."

Bella made a quick plea to hold on but he was acting on reflex. Marco couldn't believe what he was hearing. Out of a protectiveness that was wholly different than what he felt for

Bella, Marco didn't try to make himself decent. He lowered his gun and opened the door.

The cold from outside rushed in and hit his chest and legs. Marco didn't mind it. He was caught between smiling, laughing and being absolutely concerned.

"Amy?"

Amy Rossi-Johnson had a suitcase at her side, a hand on her hip and was nothing but stern.

"First of all, how dare you not call me back *or* answer your phone when I call," she nearly yelled. "Secondly—"

Amy stopped herself. Her eyebrow rose and she did a quick scan of the scene in front of her.

Marco in his boxers.

Bella wrapped in the blanket from his bed.

Clearly past normal visiting hours for just friends.

Definitely not what she had expected.

"Oh, well, if I had known I was interrupting…"

Marco groaned, realizing there was no way to spin what she was seeing. Not that he wanted to but he doubted this was how Bella had wanted to meet his sister for the first time.

"If you'd known, you'd still do it. Now get inside." Marco grabbed her suitcase. "I don't need the neighbors seeing me in my underwear too."

Amy went from maternal worry to sisterly

curiosity in a flash. She moved past him like water around rocks in a persistent stream and was on Bella in a second.

"Hi, I'm Amy. Marco's sister."

Bella, to her credit, went with the flow. Despite how red her face had turned, she held out her hand and was all polite.

"Nice to meet you! I'm Bella. Bella Greene."

Marco took the suitcase and set it down next to the couch. In any other circumstance, he knew Amy would've been ravenous for more details, but in the moment she put her hand on her chest.

"You're the one who saved him," she exclaimed. "You went with the bad guy so he wouldn't get hurt."

None of it was a question. Still, Bella nodded.

"Though, to play devil's advocate, I was the reason he was in danger in the first place."

Amy shook her head.

"I don't think so, lady. You deserve the praise I gave you and more."

Unlike Marco, his little sister was a very openly affectionate person. She believed in pats on the back, hands on cheeks and hugs that were too tight and went on for far too long. Bella being her target warranted no exception. Amy pulled her into a hug while saying thank-you.

Again, to Bella's credit, she was nothing but grace as she accepted it.

"Where's Matthew?" Marco asked, trying to distract Amy from squeezing the life out of his guest. "And why are *you* here?"

It was like she'd been slapped. His sister turned around so fast even her short hair moved at the speed.

"Matthew is at a work conference that I assured him he didn't have to leave unless I needed him to. I won't dignify your second question with an answer other than I am your sister and you were in the hospital two times in one day. Not to mention you were there because someone was trying to kill you. If that doesn't warrant your sister-bestie coming down to check on you, then I don't know what does."

Marco snorted.

"I thought you weren't going to dignify my question with an answer."

"And you're just lucky that I convinced Mom and Dad to wait to come out here next weekend and not with me instead." That annoyed sisterly affection turned quickly into a smirk. "Can you imagine if Mom and Dad walked into this? You'd never live it down."

Marco rolled his eyes, mainly because he knew that since Amy had interrupted them, he still wasn't going to live it down. She was going to tell this story at all holiday functions for the rest of their lives. Because that's what the Rossi siblings did. They loved each other wholeheartedly and they loved to tease each other wholeheartedly too.

"Can I just say that I personally am thankful that you showed up and not your parents?" Bella chimed in. "As far as first impressions go, I was kind of hoping with your parents I'd be a little more charming and a lot more clothed."

Amy laughed out loud. Marco caught himself pausing.

He'd told Bella more than he'd ever told anyone else. Not only about what happened at his past job but why exactly it hurt him so deeply. That meant a lot and he wasn't sure if she even realized how much. But he also knew that the kind of situation that they had been in the past few days, one that was high stress and danger and fear, could incite an emotional and physical connection that could go away just as quickly as it had come on.

Now that Conrad was no longer a part of the picture, how would Bella feel the next day about him? Without emotions running high. How would she feel the next week or month?

Would she really want to meet his parents or did she just feel that way because of the connection they'd shared earlier?

Marco didn't know the answers and, as Bella searched his face, he wished he did. Instead he excused himself.

"Speaking of clothes, I think I'm going to go grab some more."

"I think I'll join you," Bella tacked on, jumping ahead of him to hurry down the hall.

Amy laughed and called after them.

"And I'm going to make some coffee, because there's no way we're not talking about *everything* that's happened, Big Brother!"

FRIDAY MORNING CAME like nothing out of the ordinary had gone on the week before. Bella returned to her house and walked through it alone, trying to shake off the fear that had settled in her chest when she had first seen the message written on the mirror.

The sky darkened outside, promising eventual rain, but slowly Bella started to melt back into the warmth that her house had always made her feel. Then she took out a page from her mother's book and worked the rest of her anxiety off by doing the one thing that she could absolutely control.

She cleaned.

To the normal chores of laundry and dishes, she added a deep clean of the bathrooms and kitchen. After that, she took to her bedsheets and quilt. All the while trying not to think about Conrad Abernethy or, even, Deputy Marco Rossi.

Bella failed on both accounts but none more so than the man she'd almost spent the night with.

Bella caught her reflection in the hallway mirror and smiled. That smile brought on a blush and a giggle only meant for her. There she had been taking banana nut bread to a man who'd saved her life only to fall into his bed, then into his shower, then right back into bed again.

It had felt so right, especially after a week that had felt so wrong.

But then Amy had shown up and brought Bella and Marco back down to reality.

Then Bella had seen the look.

The look Marco had given her while standing there with his sister.

Bella's reflection frowned.

Had they moved too fast? Had danger fused them together and now without it they'd fall apart?

Bella looked away from the mirror. She gathered up the rest of her linens and marched to the laundry room.

After getting dressed, she'd excused herself from Marco's apartment, insisting that the brother and sister spend time together, considering Amy had come all the way from New York out of worry.

Marco hadn't fought her on it and only asked that she text him when she returned to her parents' house for the night. She had and his response had been a simple Good.

And then when she stopped feeling like some schoolgirl with a crush, Bella thought about Conrad.

It didn't make sense to her. His obsession? He barely paid attention to her during their date. In fact she'd even made the joke to her mother that she could have put a mirror in her chair and left and Conrad would have been perfectly happy still talking to himself *about* himself.

Was that how obsession worked?

Someone who paid you no attention suddenly couldn't do anything but?

It put another chill down Bella's spine. She was almost thankful for the distraction of someone ringing the doorbell.

Bella hurried down the hall, phone in the front pocket of her overalls, and felt the nerves tighten her stomach when she realized it was none other than Amy standing on her front porch.

"Two days in a row that I've caught you unaware," Amy greeted, laughing as she did so.

"I hope you don't mind. Marco went to work and I don't want to stay all day in his depressing apartment." She motioned around herself to the house. "I'll be honest, I'm a much bigger fan of this beauty."

Bella laughed, stepped to the side and waved her in.

"Anyone who compliments my house is surely allowed inside of it."

Amy was a study in contrasts to her brother. She was petite, wide-eyed and didn't seem to hold back when it came to talking. She graciously took a seat on the couch in the living room and got down to brass tacks without any provocation.

"I honestly thought I'd be more tired since I felt like I was in airports and flying all of yesterday but after Marco left for work I couldn't go back to sleep. I also kind of wanted to see what Kelby Creek was like on my own."

Bella took the seat opposite her on an old, worn chair that had once belonged to her grandmother. It felt as comfortable as she was starting to feel with Amy, a feat considering she still felt embarrassment from being caught in just a sheet the night before.

"I'm sure our town's past and what's happened with me the last few weeks probably hasn't given you the best impression," Bella said. "Not that any of that has been sitting well with any of us locals."

Amy surprised her with a shake of her head.

"Not to sound blunt but I didn't actually care about what happened here in town. With the corruption." She raised her hands in defense. "Not that I'm saying it doesn't matter, just that I already understood why Marco wanted to move here in the first place. He wanted to help and, from what I can tell, this town might need that. And as for you and this whole creepy stalker business, I'm not about to blame you for something a guy with issues decided to do. Plus, find me a place in this world that doesn't have at least one guy doing something absolutely creepy."

Her laugh undercut the seriousness of the topic, though Bella could see that she wasn't happy with any of it.

"What I really wanted to figure out, to really understand on my own, is what about this place has made Marco want to stay."

Bella's cheeks became hot. She wasn't exactly sure why. She tried to cover the quick change with a little laugh of her own.

"I didn't even know that he was thinking about leaving but he definitely wouldn't be the first to skip town given our history."

Amy waved her hands through the air, dismissing the thought.

"He isn't talking about leaving or anything like that but I feel like he is thinking about staying. For a while." Even though Amy didn't really know Bella and vice versa, she dropped all pretenses and became serious. "Normally I wouldn't do this to my brother, pry into his personal life. At least, not so directly. I also am not going to pretend that his job can't be dangerous, and there's not anything that would stop him from doing it. But when he called me at the hospital and then when we talked later that night, I could tell something was different about Kelby Creek. Something that was important."

Bella found herself leaning in, completely enraptured by the insights of someone so close to Marco. It was like a mirror effect—Amy leaned in a little as she continued to talk.

"I asked him last night if he had told you about our past, our family and what happened to him and his last job." She smiled. It was brief but poignant. "To say I was absolutely surprised that he had opened up to someone about that is the understatement of the century in my book. In fact I don't think he's ever told anyone the specifics of how we ended up where we are now, and that goes double for how he was completely let down by those he considered his close friends in North Carolina. But, given the fact that he did open up to you, I'm going to take that on good faith and do the same."

Amy hesitated but Bella didn't think it was because she wasn't ready to talk about whatever it was she was about talk about. Instead it was like she was trying to choose her words carefully. When she finally found them, Amy didn't break eye contact once.

"Marco thinks the reason why my husband and I moved to New York was because I was feeling nostalgic for our biological family. I wasn't. The truth was that I realized early on that Marco would spend the rest of his life just as he had up until then trying to take care of me. To protect me. I realized that he would most likely always go where I went to keep that up and, let me just say, I am so grateful to have such a great brother and I truly love him with all of my heart, but I didn't want him to do that. I didn't want him to mold his life around mine just because he felt he had to because of everything we had been through. So, my husband and I moved to the one place in the entire world that I knew Marco would never willingly live because of our past."

"New York."

Amy nodded.

"I know that kind of sounds harsh, but honestly my husband and I don't plan to live in New

York for the rest of our lives. The fact of the matter is I've been waiting for *Marco* to find the place he wants to live. Somewhere that he himself chooses without any thought or feeling of responsibility for me. And then, and only then, will Matthew and I try to find a place there too."

"You'd move to Kelby Creek if Marco decided to stay?"

Amy didn't skip a beat.

"I know it probably doesn't make sense to a lot of people to uproot their lives just to try to make a new one around a sibling, but I've seen the world be cruel to my brother and entirely undeserving of him. I have seen foster parents, biological family members that have come out of the woodwork and people who were supposed to have Marco's back let him down. And still he worries about them. About everyone, even if he won't admit it. In my opinion Marco deserves, at the very least, to be surrounded by people who care about him and want to be there because of their feelings for him."

Amy stopped, like she was ending the conversation, but Bella felt like it was just getting started.

"So, you came to Kelby Creek to check on Marco but also to scope out the town?"

Amy was smiling again, her dark eyes almost a match for her brother's.

"I came to check on him, yes. I also came to figure out what about this place made him talk like he was already growing roots." That smile turned into a grin. "And let's just say, I don't think it has anything to do with the weather."

That blush that had been turning up throughout her conversation with Amy had now moved down into Bella's stomach and become a different kind of warmth. She didn't push for any more specifics about Marco or what his sister thought about him. Instead Bella did what she felt in the moment to be right.

She laughed, smiled and stood up, raring to go.

"Speaking of the weather, would you be interested in seeing the reason why I'm wearing overalls before the rain sets in? It's only a quick drive across town."

Amy matched her energy. She jumped up, keys already in hand.

"A lady's day while Marco freaks out about what we're doing while he's stuck at work? Count me in!"

Bella got a few things, grabbed her bag and locked up the house. They were sitting in Amy's rental and heading in the direction of Justin's house within minutes.

Neither woman saw him standing outside, watching them. Neither woman had any clue that, even though he no longer had his mask, that wouldn't stop what he had planned next.

Nothing would.

Chapter Seventeen

It was a piece of paper. Harmless and plain. The words written across it? Also harmless and relatively plain.

Hello there, friend.

Marco looked up from the note Bella had given him from the tool bag that had been in her truck. Carlos was in his desk chair and looked about ready to fall asleep.

"Sorry," he said. "Probably not the best thing to greet you with. I just can't get over this case."

Carlos tapped the notebook beneath the piece of paper Marco had been staring at. They were his notes, beneath them the official paperwork he was supposed to be doing instead.

In any other case, Marco still would have procrastinated on that paperwork. Crossing the *t*'s and dotting the *i*'s. It felt like he was back in grade school with an assignment he was wondering how to make his sister do instead or, another old pain, taking a standardized test. This

time around though, he was avoiding it *because*
of what was across each paper.

This case.

Conrad Abernethy's documented stalking,
undeniable attacks and eventual death.

Marco wasn't sure about that. About any of it.

"Did you know Conrad?"

Marco leaned back in his own office chair.
They were in the bullpen at the department and
two of three who were strapped to desks doing
the more technical side of being a deputy. Detective Lovett was still out and about while
Sheriff Chamblin was dealing with a press conference on Conrad's death. Thankfully the sheriff had agreed to leave Bella's name out of his
speech and comments. Something Marco was
grateful for.

"I knew *of* him but I can't remember actually meeting him." Carlos's brows furrowed
in thought. "I might have seen him at a Super
Bowl party once, but that could be said about
the whole dang town."

Marco ran his thumb along his jaw. He was
frustrated and couldn't pinpoint one reason why.

He felt the weight of his service weapon in
his holster against his hip. His thoughts went
back to the night before. He shook his head at
himself.

"Listen, I'm not going to pretend to know you

all that well yet," Carlos said. "But I think I can swing and hit something based on how you're all scrunched up in the face. Something isn't sitting right with you. What is it?"

Marco debated on saying anything, but then he heard Bella and her claim of him having armor. Marco knew it was there and, for the first time in his life, he'd told someone who wasn't his family why it was there.

He hadn't meant to open up like that to Bella and yet, once he had, he felt no regret. Instead there was a calmness to him after. With just a look of encouragement or a soft touch to remind him that he wasn't alone, Bella had made him feel…safe.

Which was why his concern now bothered him so much.

He should have felt relief at Conrad's death. He didn't.

Instead he was bothered by it.

Ignoring that wouldn't do anyone any good, so for the second time in two days, Marco opened up to someone he hadn't planned on.

"I guess I don't feel like this thing is over." It was the first time Marco had said it out loud. Carlos took that concern and mirrored it.

"What do you mean?"

Marco motioned to the paperwork on his desk.

"There are holes," he said, simply.

"Holes."

Marco touched his own notes on top. There was a descending list of events that had happened in chronological order.

"This whole thing is like a rotted-out tree. All we did was cut off the branches but the roots are still there. The problem *seems* solved but I have a feeling that we haven't dealt with one damn root."

Carlos didn't laugh or question the clumsy analogy. Instead he jumped in.

"We found Conrad with the mask and letters that matched the handwriting on the messages Bella had been getting. Plus Conrad and Bella had a connection right before she started getting those messages."

Marco conceded to that but he still couldn't get over the feeling.

"All the leads we followed or got during the last month came to a dead end. The only reason we're saying Conrad is guilty is because of what we found in his house."

"The very damning evidence that we found in his house," Carlos interjected. "Not to mention a bullet that did him in."

Marco snapped his fingers.

"It seems like that happened—that I shot him at the storage facility—but if I had, wouldn't there have been blood?" It was something he'd already brought up right after finding Conrad. "Escaping from that building before backup arrived was his number one goal. Not cleaning up any and all traces of blood. I mean, you saw his wound. There's no way he didn't bleed somewhere after being hit."

Carlos moved his head side to side, accepting the less than concrete story they'd had to put together.

"He could have gotten lucky. You said it yourself that neither you nor Bella got a really great look at what he was wearing. He could have been layered up and that caught the blood."

Marco didn't like that answer. Just as he hadn't the first time they'd come up with it. He didn't like the unsettling feeling still there either. It's what had weighed on his gut around the time his former partner had planted evidence. Marco had picked up on something being wrong; he just hadn't figured it out until it was too late.

He didn't want to make that same mistake now. Not with Bella.

"Okay," Carlos kept on. "Let's step through the rest and see what's hanging you up. Starting with Bella and her truck breaking down and you stopping to see if you could help. You think Conrad was going to try to take her then, right?"

Marco sat straighter in his chair.

He nodded.

"There was water in her gas tank, not enough to keep her engine from starting but enough to make her break down away from her house. She also found the note in her tool bag, though she admits she hadn't opened it in a while so there's a chance it had been there longer."

"So you potentially interrupt the attempt and take her to Crisp's to wait for her dad and brother to get there. Then you don't see her until we're at the bar two weeks later."

"In between that time, we run into an unusual amount of car trouble where the gas tank and lines had been tampered with, along with a slashed tire. So I approached Bella at the bar to ask her about her truck but don't get the chance because we were called away."

"Almost everyone was that night," Carlos added. "Thank you, prank calls."

"The next day Bella comes by to finish our conversation but we're interrupted again. This time by the power going out. So we decide to get dinner instead." Marco left out the part where most of their conversation had been personal and that he hadn't actually gotten around to talking about her truck then either. "Then the next night we get the call about Jennifer Parkridge's break-in and see that only her door was broken and a plant inside along with it. We call in Bella and her family to fix it."

"And later that night you go for a run and—" Carlos clapped his hands together and made a splat sound effect.

"A guy in a Halloween mask tries to run me down, just as Bella finds the message on her bathroom mirror." Marco paused, only because he hated that part. Just like he wasn't a fan at all of the next. "Bella comes to the hospital to tell me and, during that time, someone puts water in her gas tank. Someone who wore a mask to do the deed, so getting him on camera at the hospital parking lot did nothing for us. The same *no luck* with the truck that rammed us after we left."

That truck had been turned inside out but no clue, piece of evidence or record of who owned it and where it had come from was found. There were no vehicle identification number or prints either.

And, once again, no blood.

"Then there's the fact that he had a code to the storage facility," Marco continued. "The list of people renting the units that Lovett got from the building manager didn't have Conrad's name on it. In fact he had no record of Conrad ever using any of their outside units either."

"But then we loop back to the small-town

thing," Carlos pointed out. "Who's to say he didn't get it from a friend he was helping move to speed up the process? There were a lot of people on that list and just because we didn't find a connection to Conrad, doesn't mean there wasn't one."

Marco, again, had accepted that earlier. Like Carlos said, it wasn't outside the realm of possibility in a small town like Kelby Creek.

"And then we go to see if Conrad is around and find his body, the mask and the notes with the same phrase and handwriting that Bella had gotten in his room," Marco concluded. "The back door cracked open, just like it was waiting for us to come in."

Carlos rolled his chair closer to his desk. He lowered his voice.

"You seemed okay with all of this yesterday. What changed?"

Marco had been struggling with that all night. Ever since his sister had shown up. Just like he hadn't planned on sharing with the deputy, he hadn't expected to explain in detail what he did next.

"Bella was at my apartment last night, late," he started. Carlos remained impassive but Marco bet it was a topic he'd bring up later when they weren't in such a serious conversation. "While we were talking, someone started banging on my front door. We weren't expecting anyone so I got my gun, made Bella stay back and then called through to the door to see who it was."

"Who was it?"

"My sister, Amy. She came into town because she was worried about me, but I had no idea it was her—none at all—until she said something." Marco lowered his voice and glanced down at his gun. Finally he hit the moment that had shaken his confidence in the case. "When I first heard the banging against the door, I was on my gun in seconds. Every part of me was ready, but not to defend us. I was ready to use it because I was sure it was him."

That, Carlos took seriously. His expression darkened.

"The masked man?"

Marco nodded.

"My gut yelled and told me that there was still a chance that he was coming for Bella and I needed to fight first, reason it out later."

"But it was your sister."

Marco nodded, slow.

"And I calmed down after that," he said. "I went through the facts and told myself it was over."

He looked down at his notes again.

"But it doesn't feel like it's over anymore," Carlos finished.

Marco shook his head.

"No. It doesn't."

They lapsed into a small silence. It wasn't like his feelings could compete with actual evidence.

Carlos seemed to pick up on the thought.

"Why don't we head to see Amanda?" he asked. "She'll probably be done with the autopsy by now and can give you a little more peace of mind. Plus, I wouldn't mind stopping for some food on the way back. I've already eaten half of the vending machine today."

Marco decided that was better than sitting around, brooding.

They took their lunch break and Carlos's car and headed to Haven Hospital. There were a few people bustling around the waiting room but Carlos led Marco to the elevator and down to the basement. It wasn't the first time Marco had gone to a hospital's morgue for work but it was the first time he'd had the displeasure of doing it in Kelby Creek. Though, if he were being honest, all morgues to him looked the same.

The coroner, however, did not.

Amanda Alvarez had neon pink–tipped hair and scrubs, and didn't notice them at first. When she looked up from her desk, she made a *yip* noise and put her hand to her chest.

"Geez Louise, Park," Amanda exclaimed. "Give me a one-way ticket to my own metal slab, why don't you."

Park laughed.

"Sorry, Amanda. I should have called ahead."

Amanda's surprise shifted when she looked at Marco. He wasn't sure if she remembered meeting him during his first week but she made it clear that she meant the pointed stare.

"I was about to call you."

Marco and Carlos shared a quick look.

"You were going to call me?" Marco repeated.

She nodded.

"I called Foster right before you came in. He told me to call you because of your friendship with Bella Greene."

Marco's gut was yelling. Still, he kept his voice calm.

"Why?"

Amanda stood up, came around her desk and took Carlos's hand. The deputy raised his eyebrow but let her lead him a few steps back from Marco.

"Pretend this is Conrad Abernethy," she started, focused on Marco. "The bullet that killed him landed here." She pressed her finger to a spot below Carlos's rib cage. It made him jump but she continued, unperturbed. "Now, the assumption was that he was hit from several yards away and then bled out at home after not getting seen about it."

"But you don't think that happened," Marco guessed.

She shook her head.

"He *was* shot here but it was at a closer range. And I don't think it was a through-and-through."

"I thought you said you couldn't find the bullet?" Carlos interjected. "If it wasn't in him, then it had to have gone through."

"But you didn't find it either," she returned. "Same with an impact area that would have been made after it went through him. Which got me really thinking about where this missing bullet went."

If Marco had been sitting down, he would have been on the edge of his seat.

"What conclusion did you come to?" he asked, muscles tightening in anticipation. His earlier feeling that something was off was slowly becoming worse.

Amanda put her finger back on Carlos's stomach.

"When I went to take a closer look, I noticed trauma halfway through Mr. Abernethy and then more trauma on the way out." She turned Carlos so his side was facing Marco. He made a noise but she shushed him. "I think he was shot at a much closer range, the bullet lodged inside him as he bled out and *then*—" she ran her finger from Carlos's stomach, over his side and then to a spot on his back that would have made a straight line "—someone extracted the bullet postmortem."

Marco felt his own eyes widen.

Carlos no longer cared that he was being used as a live dummy.

"Wait," Carlos started. "You think someone shot him and then took the bullet out. Why?"

Marco took a step forward, as if closer proximity would make a new truth materialize. Yet it wasn't happening. That bad feeling had expanded into an ever-growing balloon. Adrenaline was already starting to flood through him.

Because he knew.

He knew right then that he'd messed up.

That he never should have left Bella alone.

Not when he had doubt.

Not until he was 100 percent sure.

"He did it so we wouldn't find out that the bullet that killed Conrad didn't come from my gun. So that we'd think that Conrad was the one I shot at and not him. He did it so we'd leave Bella alone."

Even to Marco's ears, his voice had gone cold. Dark. Unforgiving. When he bottom-lined the terrifying reality, he knew that everything was about to get worse.

"He did it so he could try and take her again."

Chapter Eighteen

"Well, not to be that person, but I don't know why he'd want a shed." Amy was staring at Justin's house in absolute awe. "No offense to you or your business."

Bella laughed, mostly because she'd heard it before. She said as much.

"My brother, Val, can't believe it either. He said if he had *Justin money*, he'd build a pool instead. He meant to say an infinity pool but he said X-finity. You know, like the cable service." Bella snorted. "Which is why I'm pretty sure Val will never have *Justin money*."

Amy laughed and followed Bella around the house to a seldom-used worn path she and her family had made during the construction process. They didn't always use it since they were now storing their tools in his garage, but since she had no idea if Justin was home or not, she didn't think it wise to try to walk through his house with a stranger just to get to his backyard.

"And this guy won't care that we're just walking around his place during the weekend?"

Bella nodded, though she wasn't entirely confident.

"I probably should have asked but when we started building the shed, he gave us free-range of the yard. I don't think he'll mind me just popping by to show it off." Bella felt her own smile turn into a beam. "We're very proud of what we've made so far."

They cleared the house and the path curved, going downhill for a few yards before finally stopping.

Bella knew not everyone was impressed at their structures, especially when compared to the almost-mansion behind them, but she side-eyed Amy, hoping for a positive reaction. Since meeting Marco, the shed had gotten siding, a custom-built door and a roof. Plus, it had passed a few inspections. Even though they had windows, trim, the small porch and landscaping left, Bella was immensely proud of how it had turned out. More so because Justin had let them design the entire thing themselves, saying he trusted their vision.

Now Amy was smiling at the vision.

A warmth of pride spread through Bella, especially when Amy clapped.

"Holy guacamole, Bella! Did you really *build* this? Like with your own hands?"

Bella laughed again.

"Yes, but also with my dad and brother," she said. "It's a team effort when it comes to Greene Thumb and Hammer."

Amy shook her head, still smiling.

"Has Marco seen this? Surely he knows how much of a bad butt you are."

A blush, hot and true, scorched up Bella's neck and filled her cheeks. She might not have reacted so strongly to just the man's name but his sister catching her in a blanket the night before was still a fresh embarrassment.

Not only because they'd been caught, but because Bella hoped it was something that they could repeat.

That could become normal.

The two of them.

Did Marco feel the same?

She had no idea.

Bella decided not to hover around the uncertainty and instead enjoy Amy's company. One thing had been clear the night before and that was how much Marco loved his sister and vice versa. It made her want the youngest Rossi to like her as much as Bella was starting to like her.

"I've barely been here lately," Bella hedged.

Amy was persistent.

"Well, when we all have supper tonight, I'll make sure I tell him to get on that ASAP. This is seriously impressive."

Bella hadn't been aware they were doing supper but didn't question it. Instead she unlocked the padlock on the front door and gave a more in-depth tour of the structure. Amy asked questions about several things and how they were built, what came next and the vision of how it was supposed to turn out. It was exciting to have someone, especially a woman, paying such close attention. So much so that she didn't even notice at first when Justin walked up.

He cleared his throat and gave a small wave.

"Didn't mean to interrupt but I saw you out here and thought I'd see how you were doing," he greeted. Then he turned to Amy with a smile. "And introduce myself so you didn't think I was being inhospitable."

That blush came back full burn. Bella laughed through it.

"I'm so sorry, Justin. I wanted to show it off. I should have asked first."

He waved her off.

"Hey, I'm proud of this thing too. It's no sweat off my back."

"I'd be proud of it too," Amy said. "My husband and I couldn't even put together our IKEA bed frame!"

They all shared in another round of polite laughter and then Bella did the introductions. Justin, as always, was polite and engaging, the hallmarks of the businessman.

"We've been really lucky to have your brother here," he said after they'd shaken hands. "I don't know what we would do if something had happened to Bella. This town has already had too much bad in it. We don't need any more."

An expression she couldn't nail down went across Justin's face. He'd often had moments like that during the span of their friendship. Bella imagined she too would have those moments if the love of her life had died from such senseless violence like what had happened during The Flood to his wife.

Amy must have sensed that he had fallen back into a less than ideal emotion. She motioned to the shed as a whole.

"Well, I can't wait to see a picture of the finished product," she said. "I'm really bad at imagining finished products, hence my and my husband's lack of IKEA-building skills."

"I think I might be able to help with that." Justin thumbed back toward his house. "I have the sketch inside if you want to see it."

"Sketch?" Amy asked.

"We actually designed the structure ourselves and my mom sketched what the finished product is going to look like. We gave it to Justin for his okay." Bella smiled. "I didn't think you still had it."

"I wanted to hang it inside when it's all done." He shrugged. "I thought Grant would get a kick out of that."

Bella agreed her dad would.

"Well, if it's all right with everyone, I'd like to see it," Amy said. "I don't have anywhere else to be either."

"I wouldn't mind seeing it again," Bella admitted.

Justin led them up the slope of the backyard and to the patio. There were two doors. One going left to the garage and the other going into the eat-in kitchen area to the right. They followed him through into the kitchen.

"I have it downstairs in my workroom or either upstairs in my office." Justin chuckled. "I was never the most organized when it came to this house."

"You've seen the state of our tools," Bella pointed out. "Clearly you're a lot more put together than us Greenes."

They followed him through the kitchen, into the main entryway and up to a door tucked beneath one of the staircases.

"You go low and I'll go high?" he asked.

Bella's reaction was immediate. She cringed.

"Is there any way we can switch? Basements freak me out." It was the main reason she'd never gone down there before. And why she was glad that most houses in the Deep South didn't have them.

"I agree with that," Amy chimed in.

Justin smiled but hesitated enough to show that he felt something. Something that wasn't his polite, normal self.

"My wife was the same way." He seemed to shake himself and the feeling off. Then he pointed up the stairs. "First door on the left. It should be open already and either on my desk or on the cabinet behind it."

They split up and Bella and Amy made their way to the designated room. Along the way, Amy commented on how well done the inside was.

"Does he live here alone?" she asked as they walked into the office. It, like the rest of the house, was pristine and grand. Bella imagined her own cluttered and small workspace at home. Before she could stop it, she wondered what Marco had thought of her home. Had he liked it? Had he wanted a tour that didn't involve her looking for clues?

Would he like to spend time there with her?

Bella pushed all those thoughts to the side and answered Amy, hoping she hadn't noticed the pause.

"Yeah, he has since his wife passed."

Bella smiled when Amy went to snooping around Justin's built-in bookcases and the picture frames and knickknacks it housed along with the hundred or so books on its shelves.

"I don't think I could stand being in a place this big by myself," she ventured. "Though I don't think I could stand being alone anywhere to be honest. I've been with Matthew since I was fifteen. I don't think I could even function without him."

Bella felt an odd ache. For Justin and his loss and for never having a loss at all. It was a weird feeling but somehow it pointed out the emptiness she'd had for the last few years.

This time she couldn't quite shake it off. So she focused on Justin and went to the desk at the back of the room. It was cluttered. She made sure to glance at the door before she spoke.

"When I first met him, he actually wasn't all that great," she said, quietly. "He was three-whiskeys deep at our local bar and looked like he was ready to just melt into the floor. I knew what had happened to his wife and I just felt so bad for him that I had to say something. After that, my family and I became friends with him and his mother. He's seemed a lot happier lately, which is nice."

After moving the papers and work debris around on the desk to find the large sketch, Bella came up empty.

But she did find something.

They was a set of keys, hidden beneath a pile of mail. She wouldn't have thought anything of them but the keychain caught her eye. It was bright pink instead of silver, a keepsake from a breast cancer awareness fundraiser. Bella knew this because she'd gone with her dad to it to show support for one of his friends.

"You found some keys?" Amy asked, losing interest in the contents of the bookcase.

Bella nodded.

"They're my dad's. He lost them the other day when he was rushing to come see me at the hospital. Justin ended up giving him a ride."

"Why are they up here?"

It was an innocent question. One that could have had an innocent answer.

Yet Bella froze as she looked at the keys. Or, rather, the old check signed beneath it.

Then, all at once, it clicked. Just like that.

Bella went from happy, content and safe to feeling sick.

Amy was no fool.

She noticed the change right away.

"Hey, what's wrong?"

Bella put the keys down and reached for her phone. She came up short. Her cell phone was in the car.

"Call your brother," she hurried, her voice wavering and breaking. She was drowning in adrenaline, her heartbeat going from carefree and steady to terrified and panicked all at once.

Amy followed her instruction but asked why as she pulled her phone from her pocket.

"We need to get out of here," Bella hurried.

She started to move but something blocked the door.

Someone.

Amy hadn't seen him yet. She repeated her question of why.

Justin, at the very least, was polite enough to respond, despite the gun he was holding in his hand.

"Because she just realized something, didn't you?"

Amy turned and froze. Her still-locked cell phone in her hand.

"What—what's going on?"

Bella wished she could close her eyes and make it all go away, but Justin kept on, never leaving the doorway or lowering his gun. He had it trained between them but he could change his aim in an instant, if he wanted.

"Go on, Bella. We don't have to keep any secrets from each other anymore," he said, all smiles. "Tell us what you've just figured out."

Bella shook her head. Justin wasn't a fan.

He moved his aim to Amy. She didn't move an inch.

But Bella did.

She took the woman's hand in hers and held the other one up in a Stop motion.

"Don't! Please!" Bella pointed down at the desk. "It—it was the check right here. It's—it's the same handwriting as the notes."

Justin shook his head.

"I know you, Bella," he said, almost like a coo. "I know your every expression. That face you're doing now? It's the same one you do when you're trying to figure out the dimensions on something when you're working. You're calculating something and you can't calculate without more than one figure. So what's the rest? Because I know there's more than just that."

He took a step inside.

Bella lowered her hand but didn't let go of Amy's. If they weren't on the second floor, she would already have pulled the woman to and through the window if possible.

But this wasn't a movie, and they'd probably never even make it to the window without being shot first.

Bella didn't want that for Amy or herself.

She didn't want it for Marco either.

"The—the keys," she stumbled. "We figured that the only way someone broke into my house was with a key. Only—only my family has that."

She glanced down at her father's keys.

Justin seemed humored.

"But your father didn't realize they were gone until the day after you found the message. So that could have been nothing more than me finding them and holding them here until he came back." He shrugged. "There has to be something else."

There was.

Amy squeezed her hand. She was surprisingly calm.

Bella was barely keeping it together, but she answered, not knowing what it would accomplish.

"I remembered the bar. When I first met you," she managed. "I remembered that Conrad wasn't the only person I said hello to when I was nervous."

"And, can you tell Ms. Amy here how you greet people when you're nervous?"

That sick feeling in Bella's stomach only spread. Justin's smile deepened. He was proud of her and that somehow made it all worse.

Bella let out a low, shaky breath, but she answered the man all the same.

"Hello there, friend."

Chapter Nineteen

No one answered their phones.

Not Bella. Not Amy.

Neither were in his apartment and neither were at Bella's house.

Marco met Grant and Val there while Bella's mom stayed at home, hoping they'd show up there.

"Mom's car is still here," Val greeted, face darkened with worry. He pointed to the car in the driveway.

"She's been borrowing it since her truck got totaled," Grant added, huffing up to them on the front porch.

"I think she might be with my sister. Her rental is gone and she's not answering either." Marco had to move past the anger and panic at both women missing and stay on their current course of action. He pointed to the door. "No one answered but I don't have a key."

Val nodded emphatically, bringing out his

personal house key. He lived down the road from Bella and had gotten there within what felt like a minute. His father being with him had been a well-timed coincidence. It was lucky for Bella's house that they were quick. Marco had been about to break down the door when he called.

"I would have brought mine but my keys are still missing." Grant cussed low. After Marco had told Val that he needed to get inside Bella's house because she was missing, he'd underlined the urgency by saying that Conrad most likely wasn't the stalker.

Now they were all on high alert.

Val opened the door and all three spread out while calling Bella's and Amy's names. If his heart weren't beating out of his chest and his senses all sharpened to figure out what had happened to them, Marco would have taken a moment to feel something at the fact that the Greenes were calling out for his sister with just as much concern for her safety as Bella's.

But neither woman answered their calls.

The house was empty.

"The house is still locked up and her purse is gone," Marco summed up when they all made it back to the living room. Grant looked like he'd aged a decade just since the last time they'd seen each other a minute or so ago.

"So we think she left on her own?" Val asked.

"If she was taken," Marco said. "She most likely wouldn't have grabbed her purse unless her abductor needed it."

Grant shook his head.

"Her boots are gone. I think she left here without duress."

Marco gave the man a questioning look.

"Her boots?"

Val whirled around to the entryway. Marco followed. He pointed to a line of shoes against the wall. Between a pair of flats and a pair of tennis shoes was an empty space.

"She hates wearing them but said they're the only things that don't make her overalls look dorky," Val and Grant started at the same time. Her father beat Val to the punch.

"Which means she's probably wearing her overalls!"

Marco didn't get it.

"Why does that matter?"

Grant grabbed Marco's wrist and pulled him to the front door.

"Bella only wears her overalls to do chores in or to work in. Never to leave the house in—not since some old classmate of hers said she looked like a strung-out farmer in them."

Val followed, unlocking his car over their

shoulders with the remote. It honked twice, like it was picking up on their mounting urgency.

"The only reason she'd wear her boots was if she had on her overalls and the only reason she'd leave the house with both was because she was going to a jobsite," Val added on. "And the only site we have now is at Justin's."

"Bella might have wanted to show Amy the shed," Marco realized. He could work with that. He hurried along to his car. "Call Justin on the way. I'll follow."

Marco relayed where they were going to Carlos, who was meeting with Detective Lovett over at Conrad's house.

"Maybe their phones are just off and they're just fine," Carlos tried. But even as he said it, Marco heard the uncertainty in his partner's words. Especially since they'd already pointed out something that had sent chills down Marco's spine.

"Whoever did this had to know there was a possibility that we'd catch on once an autopsy was completed," Marco had said in the hospital. "Which means they had to know they had a shrinking window of opportunity until we realized we had the wrong guy."

Which meant he had a shrinking window of opportunity to take Bella.

Marco growled at his steering wheel once he was off the phone.

He should have been with her.

Now the two women he cared about most were missing.

Care about the most?

Marco didn't have time to focus on that thought.

He put pedal to the floor just to keep up with Val until they were whipping into Justin's long driveway. There was only one car there, and Val called out that it was Justin's as they all parked.

"Doesn't mean they weren't here," Marco pointed out. "Val, get Justin. Grant, show me the worksite."

The Greenes didn't waste any time. Val hustled to the front door while Grant led Marco around the house and down a path to the shed they were currently building.

If the situation had been different, Marco would have marveled at the structure. Instead he was all about the details. And one blaringly obvious detail was that Bella and Amy were nowhere to be found.

Grant paused at the door to the shed and then pushed it the rest of the way open. Aside from some work tools and ladders, nothing of interest was inside. Still, Grant looked around in silence while Marco looped around the structure to make sure he didn't find anything.

"He said—he said he hasn't seen them." Val ran up to them a few moments later. Justin was right behind in a jog.

He skipped any introductions.

"I've been on the back patio doing work since the weather's good," Justin added. "I haven't seen Bella or Amy all morning. I'm sorry," Justin said. "Is there anything I can do?"

Marco cussed this time. It was loud. The adrenaline that had been pouring in and out of him all day came back in. The urgency that was with it already had Marco moving again.

"Just call if they show up," he yelled over his shoulder. "We have to keep looking."

Justin nodded while the three of them rushed back to the cars.

Marco was cycling through everything that had happened in the last month, through everything Bella had told him that had happened over the last seven months to her, and trying to find something that might give him a lead. A place or a person or—

Marco slowed down by the hood of his car. He turned on his heel, looking for Val but finding Grant. His face was pinched, his brow drawn. His eyes focused but not on what to do now.

No. He had thought of something too.

"What?" Marco wasn't polite with the question. He was on Grant within a second, towering.

Bella's father didn't seem to mind. Instead he shook his head.

"He lied," Grant said, simply.

"Who lied?" Val asked, closing in their three-person half circle.

Grant was looking at Marco while he answered, his face severe.

"Only Val, Bella and I have the code to the lock on the door to the shed. We have never given it out to anyone. It's one of our main rules. We also always make sure it's always locked—we check it twice before we leave every time we're here." Grant shook his head. "It wasn't locked. It wasn't even closed. Bella was here today and Justin lied about it."

Marco didn't skip a beat. He turned to Val.

"Did you tell Justin that my sister was missing too?" he asked.

"Yeah. I said we were looking for her and Bella."

Marco lowered his voice, as if the massive house behind them could hear.

"But did you say her name? Did you call her Amy?"

Realization dawned across Val's face. Even before he shook his head.

"No. I just said it was your sister."

Marco's adrenaline was now a thundering weapon of destruction in his veins.

How could he have been so stupid?

"No one look at the house. Act like we're talking about our next steps." Marco followed his own instructions. He didn't even glance around at the large home. There were too many windows. Justin could be watching them for any hint that they'd caught on. If he really did have Bella and Amy, then tipping him off could make him panic.

And panic was never a good thing when hostages were involved.

"What's going on?" Val asked.

Marco pulled out his phone but kept it low. He finally figured out what his gut had been trying to get him to look at. One of the holes he hadn't even thought to fill.

"When Bella went on the date with Conrad, she said she had to get a friend to come pick her up while in the middle of it," he hurried. "I never asked, but do you know who that friend was?"

Grant was becoming red in the face.

He was angry.

"Justin."

"And since Bella never told anyone else about that, then Justin is one of the only people who knew about the connection between her and Conrad," Marco said. "And, if I had to guess, he was one of the few who knew Bella would be going to the city the first day I met her."

Grant nodded. "He even knew we were taking separate cars because we talked about it in front of him the day before."

Val seemed to finally get on board. His voice was flat as he added another nail in the coffin.

"He has a storage unit. Or had one for his wife's things after she died." His eyes were wide. "Which means he had the code to get into the building."

Marco had already been ready to act, but now?

Now he was ready to bulldoze the man who had played them all.

But he had to be smart about it.

He couldn't misstep. Not with Bella and his sister on the line.

"We need to leave."

"What?" Val said. "They're probably inside."

Marco got his phone out. He was ready to call everyone in, but not until he was sure Justin wasn't watching.

"That's why we have to leave," he said. "We can't let him know we're on to him. He could do something in a panic that we'll all regret. So we're going to drive down the road and pull off and try to hide our cars."

"What happens after that?" Grant's voice was low. A father angry and worried all at once.

Marco wished he could spell out exactly what would happen next. He wished he could tell him that they'd hide their cars, wait for backup, and then enter the house to find Bella and Amy safe and sound. That everyone would leave the house happy and healthy.

But Marco couldn't do that.

He couldn't predict what Justin might do or, maybe worse, what he'd already done. There was always the chance that if Justin was obsessed with Bella that that obsession could turn deadly.

For both her and Amy.

Marco couldn't think about that though.

Not now.

Grant and Val stared at him in nothing but acute worry for their family.

Marco might not be able to give them an exact plan and outcome but he could assure them of one thing.

"Then I get them back."

JUSTIN STEPPED AWAY from the window. He smiled.

The satisfied smirk spread wide across his

face, from one side to the other, and remained in place all the way down into the basement.

"Well, that was Deputy Rossi and the Greene family and now it looks like they're on their way to try to find you two again," he said. "I *was* hoping that I'd have more time but I guess if I've learned anything living in this town, it's that you have to work with the hand you've been given."

He went over to the middle of the room and the chair now bolted to the ground. Using the Greenes' tools over the past few weeks had sped up his reinforcement of several items in the basement. The chair, though, was his favorite accomplishment. He'd seen enough movies to know how a simple chair tipping over could ruin any plan.

That wasn't going to be him.

He wasn't going to let anything happen.

Not to her.

"I'm sure they'll be back but we'll be long gone by then," he added with some cheer.

The women didn't respond.

It annoyed him but, at the same time, he was happy for it.

They were struggling. Or, really, Bella was.

He crouched down next to her.

There was that face again.

That look of pure calculation and concentration.

She didn't even look away as he continued talking.

"This is good, Bella. This is good for you." He reached out and tucked a strand of hair behind her ear. It had come loose from her hair tie during the unfortunate fall down the stairs. "Now you get to see how this town causes nothing but pain."

He stood up and stretched, checking his watch as he did so. Justin had already done some quick math based on the women's sizes and assumed strength. They wouldn't last much longer.

Then he and Bella could start a new life away from the damned Kelby Creek.

He took another long look at the women and smiled once more.

"And, once you let go, you can feel the relief of leaving it all behind."

Chapter Twenty

Ten minutes earlier

It wasn't real.

It couldn't be.

The pain in Bella's fingers, hands and arms begged to differ.

Still, she couldn't wrap her head around what she was currently seeing.

And doing.

Amy was pale and bloody and the first thing that made sense. Their attempt to fight Justin and get the gun away from him in the office hadn't worked. Instead they'd wound up at the stairs to the basement, where Amy fell down after being grazed by a bullet. In Bella's attempt to stop Amy's fall, she'd gone down the basement stairs with her.

Bella had lost consciousness in an instant.

Amy hadn't.

Her cheeks had been tear-stained when Bella

came to, and her voice was hoarse. She'd been yelling at Justin. Then, when she saw Bella was lucid, had spoken quickly to her.

"Hold on, Bella!"

Her first thought had been that Amy's words were a rallying cry. One of emotional support. Maybe even one to take her mind off the pain and injuries she'd no doubt sustained falling down the stairs.

But then the tug had happened and Amy repeated herself with a cry.

Bella on instinct tightened her hold on whatever was in her hands. She cried out in pain. Then the details came in and she understood Amy's words weren't metaphorical. They were instructions.

That's when fear and panic had become so intense that Bella went numb.

Both she and Amy were tied up, but in very different ways. Bella's legs were bound by thick rope to a metal chair that wasn't budging despite the pull she was fighting against. Her upper body wasn't bound but her hands had been wrapped around a length of rope.

Rope that led up to the ceiling, wrapped around a pulley and then attached to Amy, wrapping around her body. Most notably her neck.

"Now, let me explain this," Justin said with nonchalance.

Bella yelled as Justin moved at her side. She realized he must have been the one to give her the rope as soon as she became conscious. One hand was still on hers. He squeezed that one and used the other to point up at the pulley above Amy.

"See, after we met, I started learning about construction as a way to impress you," he continued, as if it were a causal conversation. "Along the way, I learned how to make my own pulley systems and learned a bit about physics. That's how I made this little contraption and how I'm going to prove my point with it."

He stood up and touched the part of the rope that traveled up from Bella's hands to the ceiling.

"I've rigged this to follow a simple rule," he said. "If you don't hold up Ms. Amy's body weight, then the second she gets too much slack, the rope at the top will tighten around her neck. So tight that, I might add, she'll suffocate even if her feet make it to the floor."

Bella looked at the rope all around Amy. The rope at her wrists had already pulled out blood. The rope at her neck and upper body hadn't.

Yet.

Justin shook out his hands, flexing them when he was done.

"I'll be honest, I've been holding her up while

we waited for you to wake and, it's not an easy task. Especially since your hands were, well, hurt from your accident down the stairs."

Bella's hands were in front of her face, holding on to the rope as best she could, given Amy's bodyweight. There was blood dripping down the rope and across Bella's hands.

That's why it hurt more than it would have, she realized.

Her palms were open wounds trying to hold slipping rope with the weight of a body at its end.

"I don't understand," Bella said, voice breaking. "Why are you doing this?"

Justin pointed to Amy. She glared.

"Because she's a lesson. One I'm proving to you. One—"

He cut himself off and pulled his phone out. He wasn't been happy with whatever he saw.

"I'll be right back and we can discuss this further." He bent down next to Bella and smiled. "Don't worry. I'm doing this for us. For you. Once this lesson is done, we can go and never come back. Just remember, if you let go of that, even a little, it's lights-out for our guest."

Justin left them in the basement alone with that. Amy spoke first, angry.

"*He* cut your hands."

"What?"

Amy let out a frustrated, shaky breath.

"He said you hurt them in the fall but after he strung me up, he got a knife from his pocket and cut your hands open. He did it so it would be harder for you to hold on."

The mention of the cuts seemed to make the pain that much worse. Bella winced as the rope slipped a little. Amy in turn dropped just that much.

"Oh, God. I—I'm sorry," Bella said, tightening her grip through the burn. "It—it's also slippery."

Amy shook her head, slowly.

"None of this is your fault. It's all his. Don't you let him make you forget that."

Bella didn't say so then but she was already struggling to keep Amy up. Every part of her was pounding in pain, including her head. It swam, never mind the weight on the other side of the rope. Bella was a small woman and being completely tied to a chair, unable to get a better stance at least, made everything worse.

"I just don't understand why he's doing this," Bella let out, tears threatening to push through. "If he's obsessed with me, then why is he torturing us?"

"I don't know but—but he definitely wants you to be the one to kill me." Amy didn't mince her words. "He said he wanted you to learn now and not later like Carla had? Who's Carla?"

That confused Bella even more.

"His late wife," she said, trying to piece together what lesson she needed to learn and why Carla had learned hers later. "Some corrupt law enforcement staged a shoot-out and she got caught in the cross fire. But—but I don't get how that has anything to do with me or this nightmare scene."

Amy didn't have the answer either.

So they tried to do what they could before Justin came back.

It wasn't a lot.

Amy was a good foot off the ground and, based on the small slip and how the rope had tightened, Bella knew she couldn't slowly lower the woman down. She also couldn't get free from her chair to grab her or help. Even if she could support the woman's weight with one hand and use her other to try to untie herself, it wouldn't work. Justin had knotted the rope holding Bella beneath the chair. She couldn't reach it without getting up. As for anything around her in reach, there was nothing.

The basement wasn't opulent or large like the rest of the house above it, but there was enough space around them to keep both women isolated.

"The only thing I can use is him," Bella decided once they'd listed off all the things they couldn't do in quick succession. "If he gets close enough, maybe I can grab him with one hand and try to get something off him to get myself free."

Amy seemed to like that idea but there was no disguising the anger there. Behind those eyes that matched her brother's to a T. She didn't have to say his name for Bella to know whom she was talking about next.

"This will destroy him," she said, quiet but filled with rage. "If I die and you're taken, he'll burn the whole world down until it's done. And I don't know if he'll be able to come back from that." Amy's eyes widened and that anger quickly turned to determination. "Bella, if this doesn't work out, you have to fight and then when Marco comes, you have to make sure this all doesn't consume him. Okay?"

"You're not going to die," Bella promised.

Amy wasn't willing to hear that.

"But if I do—"

But Bella was just as stubborn.

"You're *not* going to die," she said. "We're going to get out of this somehow. You'll see."

"Bella, look up at this thing I'm attached to," Amy said. "This guy learned how to and then built a pulley system just for this purpose. He's been planning this for a long time. And he's clearly good at it."

Bella shook her head. She heard Marco's words in her head and added on to them.

"We weren't supposed to be here today," she said. "Which means he acted on impulse. And when you act on impulse, you get sloppy. And when you get sloppy, you're just asking for a man like Marco to figure out that plan and ruin it."

At that, Amy smiled.

But then footsteps sounded on the stairs and Justin came in, cheerful.

Bella ignored him the best she could while he spoke. Focusing instead on two things: holding on to the rope no matter how much it was hurting her hands and starting to make her arms shake, and any opening she could use to try to grab Justin and save Amy.

After tucking a piece of hair behind her ear, though, he moved out of range. Then he spoke about the relief of letting go and Bella couldn't keep quiet anymore.

"What are you talking about, Justin?" She heard her own struggle to hold the rope come through her voice. She pushed on, finding his gaze and hoping it would keep her pain on the back burner long enough to buy them more time. Or just enough conversation to get him closer to her again. "I don't understand why you're doing this or whatever lesson you're trying to teach me. How can it work if I don't understand it?"

Justin, who she'd always thought was a good guy dealt a bad hand, now looked like a crazed man who was unaware of just how far he'd thrown the deck of cards out the window. But, at the very least, he seemed to care about what she had to say. He even considered a moment before he answered. Bella was surprised at how lucid he was.

"Did I ever tell you I drowned here? In this town and in that awful creek?" He didn't pause for a response. "I was in high school and had gone out with some friends for a late-night round of truth or dare and the next thing I know I'm gulping for air and sinking to the bottom of that disgusting water." His face contorted into anger. "I was saved but after that, not only did I hate the creek, I hated the town."

Justin took a step closer, maybe four feet from her. Bella tightened her grip on the rope. She held in a wince from the pain the best she could. Justin kept talking, unaware of it or he simply didn't care.

"I was ready to leave but then I met Carla," he continued. "Now, she—*she* loved this town. Loved it so much that she said she knew she wouldn't be happier anywhere else in the entire world. Made me buy this house when I could have given her a castle anywhere else. But no. It was Kelby Creek or die for her."

This time, he caught Bella off guard and laughed. It was unkind.

"If she had only known that would end up becoming the choice for her, then I'm sure we could have been happy anywhere else. But she dug in her heels and won every fight we ever had about leaving."

Justin took a step closer. Instead of moving his gaze around the room, now he focused on Bella only. Her arms started to shake at the strain of holding Amy up.

Now she was trying not to cry.

She didn't want to give him the satisfaction.

"Then she got caught in this town's muck and, with her last words, admitted that I was right. That we should have left." Every emotion drained from him. It was such an alarming change in tone that Bella became afraid to look away. His voice was hard. Steel against the road. "And she didn't even know why she died. She didn't know that this town killed her for money of all things. Money I had. Money I could have given them instead of them taking her. But no. That's not how this godforsaken town works, is it?"

He moved to Amy with such speed that Amy yelled out. Justin jabbed his finger into the blood on her side where the bullet had grazed her. She cried out again.

"Everything this town did and I have to sit back and watch them walk around like nothing ever happened? I have to watch more people like her brother come in and try to redeem this place?" He laughed. Goose bumps spread across Bella's body as a violent chill went through her at the sound of just how far gone he was. "This town doesn't *deserve* redemption."

He shoved Amy. Not hard enough to hurt her but enough to make holding her still impossible. The rope slipped over an inch. Bella yelled as she tried to stop it from falling farther. The pain and blood all over her hands was a nightmare, but not as much as seeing the rope around Amy's neck tighten. She started to cough.

"Then why me? Why take me? What lesson are you trying to teach?" Bella cried out. She needed him to focus on her. She needed him to get closer.

The question, at the very least, distracted him.

Justin stepped away from Amy. She could still breathe but there were tears in her eyes.

"Because, Bella, the moment I made the decision to *finally* leave this awful place, you showed up. On the barstool next to me. Smiling." At that, his rage switched back to unsettling cheer. *"Hello there, friend."*

He finally walked to her, crouching down between both women. He put his hands on her knees and smiled.

"That's when I knew. That's when I knew I had to save you from it all. But not before showing you how much this place can hurt. How much bad it can bring. I had to give you pain so you could see how good life can be without it. Without this town."

He was so close now. Leaning in, almost like he was going to kiss her.

Bella wanted nothing more than to get far, far away from him. But she needed that closeness.

She needed him near.

So she goaded him.

She wanted him to get sloppy again.

"But then Marco showed up and confused me, didn't he?" Bella tilted her head to the side. Justin mimicked the motion. His eyes were glazed over, lost in his own obsession and anger. She nodded slowly. He did that too.

"I had a better plan. Poetic too. I was going to take you and make a statement and show you pain through your father. Not like this but I had a way."

Bella swallowed her own rage. She needed him just a little closer.

"But Marco messed that up and you had to improvise," she spelled out.

He nodded.

"He even messed up my plan B." Justin's eyes dropped to her lips. Bella held in every urge she had to gag. "But now look at us. You're about to learn your lesson and then we can finally leave this place together."

Bella didn't want to but she looked away from the man. Only for a moment and only for one reason.

Amy met her stare with an absolute calm. Without saying a word, the youngest Rossi knew exactly what Bella was asking.

And she was ready for it.

Her voice was a rasp but it was clear.

"Do it."

Justin never saw it coming.

Bella knew she couldn't hold the rope with one hand, just like she knew she couldn't do that much damage to him with just one either.

So she channeled the extremely familiar motion of coiling up an extension cord. Something she did every workday when they were done using the saws and cleaning up.

This time though, instead of wrapping up a cord to keep it neat, Bella used the last of her strength to try and wrap the rope around his neck.

Justin was too close to escape the move. Bella yelled as she jerked the rope down. A new wave of adrenaline was the only reason she got the rope around his neck once. She pulled down as hard as she could.

It wasn't enough.

Justin's hands went to his neck, putting his fingers beneath the rope with ease. Once there he one-handedly pulled it away while using his other hand to hit Bella across the face.

It hurt but she stayed focused through the pain.

She still was holding the rope. If she didn't keep that hold, then Amy was done.

Though her good intentions weren't enough.

Not compared to Justin's rage-filled strength.

He tore the rope from her hands and stood.

"I guess I'll have to teach you the lesson myself."

Everything happened in an instant.

Bella screamed as Justin let go of the rope.

Amy made an awful sound.

A gunshot went off, so loud that Bella felt it in her bones.

Justin fell back, away from Bella.

She didn't have time to look to see who had done it. Though she knew in her heart who was there.

Instead she scrambled for the rope and caught it as Amy went red in the face.

"Marco, the rope!"

He was fast. He was between them as quickly as he had appeared.

Marco grabbed the rope and pulled it down like it was the easiest thing he'd ever done. Amy let out a gasp as the move allowed her slack.

Bella wanted to cry in relief but then she heard her father.

"Gun!"

Bella turned in time to see that Justin hadn't hit the ground. Even though blood was coming out of his shirt at the chest, he was still standing. And he was still moving, right toward the cabinets along the far wall.

And the gun he'd used on them earlier that was on top of those same cabinets.

Bella watched in muted horror as Justin grabbed the weapon and spun around to face them.

She had no way to protect herself. No way to protect Marco or the sister he loved with all of his heart. No way to keep her father, who was somewhere behind them, out of harm's way.

Bella couldn't do anything except watch as he took aim at her.

But what a sight it ended up being.

Marco let go of the rope with one of his hands. Instead of Amy dropping, he pulled the rope with him as he took one giant step to the side, and she lifted all the way to the ceiling. The sheer strength seemed to ripple out and across the man as he used his new position to do the unthinkable.

Marco used his body as a shield for Bella just as Justin took his shot.

Bella and Amy yelled out as the shot hit.

Marco's body folded in as the bullet struck somewhere in his upper body. Bella couldn't see.

When the second shot sounded, she was sure that it was all over for the three of them.

It took her far too long to realize that the third shot had come from behind her.

"He's down!" It was her father's voice. He came into view behind Amy, gun raised and aimed still on Justin. "Val, grab the rope!"

Bella felt that numbness again. Her family's voices became background noise. All she could focus on was the man still standing in front of her.

Marco didn't speak.

He also didn't let go of the rope.

He just continued to stand there, being his sister's savior and Bella's shield.

Her very own set of armor.

Chapter Twenty-One

"Well, I hate to say it, but I think that's going to scar a little worse than the last thing I saw when I was in here."

Marco rubbed the sleep from his eyes and, for a moment, forgot where he was.

Then the dull ache of pain meds wearing off hit him, along with the fluorescent lights above, the hardness of the bed below and the man beside the bed in a chair next to him.

Grant motioned to the second bandage just below his collarbone. Getting shot had hurt like hell but he'd thanked his lucky stars the second it had happened that it had happened.

The fact that it wasn't a through-and-through only made the news better.

If either hadn't happened, then Bella might have been in his place. Or worse.

And Marco definitely wouldn't be looking at a smiling Grant Greene right now.

"I heard chicks dig scars," he said with a

chuckle. "Though I'm hoping two will be enough. Not a fan of being a frequent flyer at this hospital."

Grant laughed.

"I'm sure I'm not the Greene you were hoping to see when you woke up either," he teased.

Marco shook his head.

"No offense," he joked back.

Grant laughed again and waved him off.

"None taken."

Marco glanced at the love seat next to his chair. There was a sheet on it with a folded blanket and a pillow on one cushion but no woman who had spent the last two days there. Grant let him take a moment before speaking again. His tone shifted into the more serious.

"Last time it was just me and you in here, I wasn't sure what kind of man you were," he started. "But after what you told me, I thought I had a good sense of who you were. A good man with good intentions. Someone I didn't mind hanging around with my only daughter." Grant cleared his throat. Marco heard the break in his voice but didn't address it. He let the man say his peace. He would *always* let the man say his piece. Not only had Grant Greene shot Justin, in doing so he'd saved Marco's, Amy's and his daughter's lives. Marco could try to pay the older man back for the rest of his life and still never come close.

"But then—then I saw you make a decision without time to even think about it," he continued. "And then I really saw you. A great man. And, for what it's worth, a great man who I'm extremely proud of."

Marco hadn't expected that, especially since Grant, Valerie and Val had spent the first half hour of his recovery time going over and over how grateful they were for what he'd done to save Bella.

Marco also hadn't expected how much he felt at the words now.

"It's worth a lot," he said, simply. "Thank you."

Grant cleared his throat again and nodded. The older man had managed to avoid any injuries but the stress at what had happened, the anger at Justin, it had made him tired. It had made them all tired.

But time would help with that.

Time and the fact that Justin Hastings was, and forever would be, gone.

He'd bled out before Carlos and his backup could arrive. Both Marco's bullet and Grant's had managed to do equal damage. Amanda had already stopped by to tell Marco that there was no way to know which one had killed him first.

That, in a weird way, felt poetic. The two men who would take a bullet for Bella had given one each to the man who had tried to take her away from them.

Now those men were tired and ready for everything to settle back down.

Grant stood and was back to smiling.

"Bella should be here soon," he said. "She and your sister should be back from the airport any minute now with your parents."

"Ah, so you got stuck with babysitting duty?"

Grant chuckled.

"Better to watch you audition for *Sleeping Beauty* than be stuck in another conversation about renovating your home versus buying it new between Val and your brother-in-law. They haven't quit since Matthew came into town the other day. I've watched paint dry as a part of my job and found more joy in that."

Marco couldn't help but laugh at that.

"But now that you're up, want to watch the game with me?" Grant grabbed for the remote, already turning the TV in the corner on. "It's a rerun of Auburn's dang Kick Six but it's better than another round of *Family Feud*. You and Bella smoked me on that last night."

Marco assured him that he didn't mind and thought that maybe one day he'd tell Grant just

how much such a simple request meant to someone like him.

Someone who had always wanted a big family.

Someone who had always wanted to feel love
without the worry of it going away.

But, for now, Marco decided to save that detail for his speech when he asked Grant for his
daughter's hand in marriage.

Because, as Marco had already figured out,
that's exactly what he was going to do. Just not
until he asked his mother for his grandmother's ring.

"Hey, you better pay attention to this game,"
Grant piped in when Marco got lost in his
thoughts about the future. "This game is a big
topic at Thanksgiving *and* Christmas every
year."

Marco laughed.

"Yes, sir."

IT WAS BEAUTIFUL. Despite everything, it really
was beautiful.

"Are you sure you made this?"

Bella rolled her eyes and turned to Marco
with a smirk already up.

"You keep talking like that and I'll take back
my *third* impression of you," she warned. It
made the man laugh.

"You've already admitted you like me, and you can't take that back. So—" Marco wrapped his arm around her and gently pulled her against his side so they were both still facing the whole reason they'd made the trip. He bent down and placed a kiss against her hair "—you're stuck with me."

A month ago Bella would have worried that the movement was too much for his bullet wound but in the time between then and now, he had recovered fully.

"As long as being stuck with you means we can grab some food tonight at Crisp's, I'm in."

Marco agreed that could definitely happen, then they both quieted again.

The shed behind Justin's house was finally done.

Some people didn't understand why Bella, Val and her father had wanted to finish it but Marco had never been one of them. One late night, in the dark and beneath the sheets, Bella had told him why it meant something to her despite what Justin had done.

"He wasn't wrong," she'd said, though she'd been quick to continue. "Justin, I mean. He wasn't wrong about Kelby Creek in part. It's hard not to remember what happened to Annie McHale, just as it's easy to forget that the damage and pain didn't stop with her and her family. She was just the first. After her, it all just spread." Bella had shaken her head within Marco's embrace. "I never even thought to wonder what it must have felt like for Justin to walk around this town—to see you or anyone with a badge—and just be expected to be okay."

She'd sighed. Marco had stroked her hair.

"I guess, no matter how it turned out, I feel like finishing the shed is the smallest of ways to honor the part of him that was there before Carla died. Have something that was made with love there for the next person who moves in to enjoy at least."

"That sounds like a good plan to me," Marco had said. "I can even help if you want me to. Though I stand by being awful with building things."

Bella had been learning that Marco surprising her was just par for the course with the man. Just as he'd supported the idea of her finishing the shed with her family, he'd helped her pull some strings to get Justin's body buried in a cemetery just outside the town limits since, it turned out, Carla was buried alongside her parents in the local one and there was no room left for him. At the very least, they'd helped Justin finally make it out of Kelby Creek.

"Okay, Dad and Val already got all the pictures for us earlier," Bella said after a while. "I think I'm ready to go now."

Marco took her hand and together they used the old, worn path to go back to Bella's new old truck. It wasn't the same as the one she'd had before but she was starting to fall for it all the same.

The man who held the door open for her when they got up to it?

Well, she had a sneaking suspicion that she'd fallen for him the moment he'd offered her a ride in the rain.

"Okay, so we're doing Crisp's tonight, but what about until then?" he asked, pulling her against him before she could get inside the truck. "As a reminder, Amy and Matthew will be back in town tomorrow to look at that house Val wants them to buy and, as your dad says, listening to Matthew and Val talk shop is going to drain us of our life force. *So* is there anything you want to do this afternoon with just the two of us?"

It had been an innocent question.

Bella knew that because she'd heard many a not-so-innocent question from the man.

Yet she couldn't help but grin up at him.

"I can think of a few things."

Marco threw his head back in laughter. When he was done, she knew she'd gotten him.

"Give me the keys and I can get us back to the house in two minutes flat," he said. "I can even call ahead so no one stops us. Carlos owes me anyway since he enjoyed the date I set up for him and Amanda. He'll look the other way if he sees us speeding home for a good cause."

Bella didn't say it but hearing Marco call her house their home felt better than any tumble beneath the sheets would.

Though she wasn't about to turn down one of those either.

She tossed him the keys, pulled him in for a deep kiss and broke it with a laugh.

"Then why are we sitting around here wasting time, Deputy?"

Marco pulled her back to him. This time the kiss was longer, deeper. One that Bella melted against.

When they parted, she sighed.

Marco ran a thumb along her cheek and smiled.

"It's never wasted time when I'm with you."

Bella could have lived in that moment for a long while, but life wasn't about staying in one moment. It was about living through all the good, bad and in-between moments.

If you were lucky, living those with someone good by your side.

And, as Bella felt the warmth of Marco's

hands on her waist, lips still warm where his had pressed against hers, she knew she sure was lucky.

* * * * *

Look for the next book in Tyler Anne Snell's The Saving Kelby Creek series when Surviving the Truth *goes on sale in September 2021.*

And don't miss the first book in the series:

Uncovering Small Town Secrets

Available now wherever Harlequin Intrigue books are sold!

Get 4 FREE REWARDS!

We'll send you 2 FREE Books plus 2 FREE Mystery Gifts.

Harlequin Romantic Suspense books are heart-racing page-turners with unexpected plot twists and irresistible chemistry that will keep you guessing to the very end.

FREE Value Over $20

Get 4 FREE REWARDS!

We'll send you 2 FREE Books plus 2 FREE Mystery Gifts.

Harlequin Presents books feature the glamorous lives of royals and billionaires in a world of exotic locations, where passion knows no bounds.

FREE
Value Over
$20

Get 4 FREE REWARDS!

We'll send you 2 FREE Books plus 2 FREE Mystery Gifts.

FREE Value Over $20

Both the **Romance** and **Suspense** collections feature compelling novels written by many of today's bestselling authors.